Untethered

R.A. THORN

REAMSPINNER
PRESS

Published by
DREAMSPINNER PRESS

5032 Capital Circle SW, Suite 2, PMB# 279, Tallahassee, FL 32305-7886 USA
http://www.dreamspinnerpress.com/

This is a work of fiction. Names, characters, places, and incidents either are the product of author imagination or are used fictitiously, and any resemblance to actual persons, living or dead, business establishments, events, or locales is entirely coincidental.

Untethered
© 2015 R.A Thorn.

Cover Art
© 2015 Anna Sikorska.
Cover content is for illustrative purposes only and any person depicted on the cover is a model.

ISBN: 978-1-63216-883-2
Digital ISBN: 978-1-63216-884-9
Library of Congress Control Number: 2014922087
First Edition April 2015

Printed in the United States of America
∞
This paper meets the requirements of
ANSI/NISO Z39.48-1992 (Permanence of Paper).

For all my LJ friends who have given me so much love and support over the years.

CHAPTER ONE

THE DOCTOR pressed his stethoscope to Frankie's chest and ordered him to take a deep breath. Frankie did so, wishing they would turn up the heat a little in the exam room. He had goose bumps all over his arms.

"Now let it out," the doctor said, and Frankie expelled the air from his lungs. "Good."

The doctor looped the stethoscope back around his neck and picked up a tongue depressor from the metal cart hosting all his instruments. He held the wooden stick poised between his fingers, like a conductor's baton. "Open up."

Frankie stared at the ceiling as the doctor pressed down on his tongue, peering into his throat with a little light. He had already had a physical when he registered at his local draft board, but the officials seemed intent on making sure no inferior specimens slipped past their screenings. The Army Air Forces only took the best.

The doctor stepped back, then made a note on his chart. "You could stand to gain a little weight, son, but otherwise you're in good form. I just have a few questions on your mental state." He gave Frankie a reassuring smile.

Frankie returned it weakly.

"You're from Idaho, correct?" the doctor asked.

"Yes, sir. A little town not far from Pocatello."

Perhaps sensing Frankie's nervousness, the doctor smiled again, pen relaxing in his fingers. "How do you like California?"

"It's swell, sir. A lot warmer than back home."

The doctor chuckled. "I imagine so. And how have you been feeling? Not depressed? Not homesick?"

"No, sir." Frankie had never been out of Idaho—trips to Boise had been his biggest excitement, but the war changed a lot of things.

1

Now here he was in Santa Ana, California, at an Army airbase, hundreds of miles from his dad's ranch in Idaho. And if all went well, soon he'd be up in the sky piloting a fighter plane over Germany or Italy or maybe even the tiny islands in the Pacific that loomed large in the news reports.

"Good, good." The doctor made another note on his chart. "Are you ever bothered by nervousness?"

"Uh, no." Frankie tried to ignore his pounding heart. He wasn't nervous exactly, but he didn't like answering all these questions.

"Do you often have nightmares?"

"Not often, I guess. Once in a while."

The doctor nodded. "Do you have siblings?"

"Yes. Two older sisters and a younger brother." It would be tough for his parents with only Colin left to help manage the ranch, since Helen and June were both married and no longer lived at home. They'd have to hire a few more hands to look after the sheep, and money was always tight. But neither his mother nor father had said a word against his enlisting. "Proud of you, son," his father had said, clapping him on the shoulder when Frankie told them he'd joined the Air Forces.

"And you get along with your siblings?" the doctor persisted.

"Well... yes," he said haltingly, thinking of the many shouting matches with his sisters and the pranks he had pulled on his brother.

The doctor laughed. "I have a brother myself. It's all good, clean fun." He gave Frankie another smile. "Your parents are alive?"

"Yes."

"Do you like girls?"

"Yep."

"Have you ever engaged in sexual intercourse?"

Oh God. Frankie really wished he could put his clothes back on. "Um, no."

The doctor gave him a stern look. "You'll be hearing a lecture this week on the menace of venereal disease. I want you to promise you'll pay attention."

"Yes, sir."

"Excellent." The doctor smiled again and scratched his signature onto a form. "Now get dressed and move along. I've got a long line waiting out there. Take this to the office at the end of the hall."

"Yes, sir." Frankie hopped off the exam table. He dressed quickly, still in his civvies but one step closer to a uniform.

Out in the hall, he walked past the crowd waiting to be examined, and joined the next line of guys in front of the room the doctor had directed him toward. So far, the Army had consisted of one long line after another.

"Think we've been prodded and poked enough?" the guy in front of him said.

Frankie shoved his hands into his pockets. "More than enough."

"No arguments from me. They even check to see if you're a fairy, sticking that thing down your throat. I choked, of course," the guy added. Then, seeing Frankie's look of confusion, he explained, "The tongue depressor. A fag wouldn't choke, see? They're used to sucking on things."

The guy laughed, and Frankie mustered a smile in return, but his palms started sweating. He'd thought it had been only the one question: *Do you like girls?* But if it had been more—and, oh Christ, he hadn't gagged. He'd just sat there with the tongue depressor in his mouth. But the doctor hadn't said anything.

Frankie swallowed, mouth dry, glancing down the corridor. Maybe the doctor would tell the MPs first, just in case Frankie tried to make any trouble. Maybe any second now they'd be coming to arrest him.

"I'm Roy, by the way," the guy said.

"Frankie," he replied. Clearing his throat, he looked back over his shoulder again.

Roy stretched and bounced on his toes. "So when do you reckon the first dance is going to be held? Because the girls back in my hometown were khaki-whacky—wouldn't look at anyone who wasn't in uniform. But if you were...." He whistled. "I imagine the gals out here aren't much different."

Frankie nodded vaguely. What should he do if they did arrest him? God, what would he say to his parents if he got sent back home?

"I was reading the paper today," Roy continued, unperturbed by Frankie's silence and leaping to a new subject like a magpie spotting bugs in the grass, "and what I want to know is whose idea it was to make Italy so blamed long? We invade in September, and now it's November and we're still inching our way up toward Rome. At this rate it will be after Christmas before we've driven the Nazis out. And if they're putting up this much of a fight now, imagine what taking France is going to be like."

The line moved forward, and Roy took a step, still talking. "The Pope's there, right? So you'd think God would've planned things a little better, that's all I'm saying." He frowned and took a closer look at Frankie. "You okay? Granted, it wasn't the funniest joke, but usually people crack a smile at least."

"I'm fine. Just... sick of waiting in lines." Frankie was trying to remember the doctor's tone of voice. Had it changed? Had he been lying when he said Frankie checked out?

"Me too. Me too." Roy suddenly yelled over Frankie's head, "Hey, George! Don't tell me they let a wimp like you pass the physical."

A guy with red hair who had just joined their line gave him the middle finger.

Roy chuckled. "That's George. Met him this morning on the train here. Say, you got a smoke?"

Frankie shook his head. "Sorry." He took a deep breath, trying to calm his racing heart. Maybe Roy had just been joking about the tongue depressor.

Roy shrugged and took another step forward. "I'll mooch some off George if this line ever hurries up and moves. What are they doing up there? Asking everyone to recite their life history or something?"

Frankie kept anxiously scanning the uniformed personnel who surrounded them. But none ever singled him out, and gradually he began to relax.

Still, he wished he had just gagged on that damn stick. It wasn't like he'd ever sucked a cock before.

Though he'd wanted to plenty of times.

Yeah, that was the kicker.

He wanted to.

When he went to enlist two days after his eighteenth birthday, he'd been nervous as hell, sure the draft board would somehow know he was queer, even though they were all locals, men Frankie had been acquainted with his whole life. But no flags had been raised. Today he'd thought he was in the clear once he lied and said he liked girls. It wasn't even really lying, because he did like girls, just not like that.

He had to be more careful. The last thing he wanted was to be slapped with an undesirable discharge and sent home. He would never be able to face his mother—his *father*. Christ, it would be a disaster. Besides, he wanted to fight and do his part in this war.

The line inched forward. Frankie finally drew close enough to see they were issuing uniforms and having problems finding the right sizes. At last it was his turn, and he collected the stack of olive drab fabric the harassed clerk handed to him. Taking a deep breath, he headed off in the direction of the barracks. No one shouted at him to stop. No posse of stern MPs surrounded him. He'd made it. From here on out, he'd concentrate on his training and keep his guard up. No one would ever have to know.

THE BARRACKS looked like they had been hastily constructed at the beginning of the war during the rapid mobilization that followed Pearl Harbor. Now, almost two years later, the paint was beginning to fade, and Frankie discovered a loose board by his bunk that let in a cold draft. After depositing his stuff on the scratchy blanket, Frankie focused on his bunkmate, who, with studied care, was tacking the photo of a girl up onto the wall. He was a little on the short side, muscular, and had pretty blue eyes, a lighter color than Frankie's.

5

Frankie stuck out his hand. "I'm Frankie Norris. That your gal?"

"Pete Norwood." He shook Frankie's hand. "And yes, this is Betty. She's a looker, ain't she?"

"Sure is." It was true. Betty had curly hair and a real nice smile. Frankie shifted, feeling nervous again. Maybe he should clip some girl's photo out of a magazine and pretend she was his girlfriend. Too bad he'd never gotten a photo of Ruth Baxter, the girl he'd dated briefly back in high school in an attempt to prove he was just like all the other guys.

"We're going to get married soon as this war is over." Pete smoothed the picture with his thumb.

Frankie nodded and tried to change the subject before Pete started asking him about his own nonexistent marriage plans. "Where are you from?"

"Boise."

"Yeah?" Frankie grinned. "I'm from a little town east of Pocatello. What are the odds, two boys from Idaho landing together?"

Pete laughed. "Pretty long, I'd say. So, what made you pick the Air Forces?"

Nerves beginning to dissipate, Frankie hopped onto his bunk and leaned back, staring at the ceiling. Sure felt nice to be off his feet after standing in all those lines. "I've wanted to fly ever since fifth grade, when my parents took us to an air show. Never thought I would, though, until the war. I thought I'd have to settle for motorcycles or breaking broncs."

"Daredevil, huh?" Pete fished a pack of cigarettes from his pocket and offered one to Frankie.

"Thanks." His mother had never let him smoke near the house, but he had sometimes snuck off after school with his friend David to have a purloined cigarette behind the gym. "I guess maybe I am a daredevil. Mostly I just like things that go really fast," he added with a grin.

"I heard they start you out in dinky little planes that got left behind in the last war."

Frankie shrugged. "They'll still be planes."

Pete stretched out too, although a good inch or two remained between his feet and the end of the mattress. That was another of Frankie's worries—that he would prove too tall to fit comfortably in the cockpit. "Seems like you started growing when you turned thirteen and never stopped," his mother always said, reaching up to pat his cheek and then making him bend down so she could plop a kiss on his forehead.

"I've never flown before, either," Pete continued. "I'm kinda—well, I hope I don't get airsick on my first flight."

"I've heard most people get over it, if you do."

"Maybe." Pete sighed. "Wouldn't be surprised if I end up in the infantry, though."

Frankie's best friend, David, had gone into the infantry. They'd enlisted together three weeks ago on October 5, two days after Frankie's eighteenth birthday and about a month after David's. "I could never cut it as a pilot, Frankie," David had said when Frankie protested his choice yet again. "You know I couldn't, not with the way I get nervous just climbing up a ladder. 'Sides, I'll get over there real soon—sooner than you will. I'll take care of the Nazis and Japs while you're still stuck in your fancy flying school."

He'd smiled, and it had been the first real smile he'd given Frankie since the previous night, just before Frankie had summoned the nerve to confess he was queer, and David had gone horribly silent.

"You don't like girls?" David repeated hesitantly, staring at Frankie.

"That's what I just said." His heart was going a mile a minute, his mouth dry.

"You mean you want to...." David trailed off, and there was a full minute of awkward silence.

Frankie didn't know where to look, so he settled for pressing his fork in the strawberry pie crumbs on his plate. His ma had made it for them, as this was their last night home.

"So you never guessed?" Frankie asked at last.

David shrugged unhappily. "Maybe. I don't know." He scowled. "Why'd you have to bring it up now, for Christ's sake?"

7

Frankie pressed his fork down harder. "Anything can happen in a war, right? And I... wanted you to know." Sighing, he set the fork down and crossed his arms. "It felt wrong to keep lying to you."

"Do your parents know?"

Frankie shook his head. "You won't tell them?"

"Of course not." David had fallen silent again and then finally said he needed to get back home because the train was leaving early the next day.

Frankie had nodded and watched him go.

So when David had smiled at him and made a joke the next day, Frankie had been so relieved, thinking maybe things were right between them again. "Yeah, well, you just be careful," he had told David, raising his voice over the sound of a train arriving at the station. "And write to your ma 'cause you know she'll worry." David was terrible at keeping in touch. One summer he'd gone off to stay with an uncle in Montana, and Frankie had heard from him a grand total of once in three months. "She can let my mother know, and then she can let *me* know, so I can rest easy that you haven't gotten your ugly mug blown up." Then he had tugged David into a hug, there on the platform waiting for the trains that would take David one way and Frankie another.

David had gone stiff and still. Frankie released him quickly, his face burning.

"Sorry," he muttered.

David had shrugged and not said anything. Three minutes later he was on the train, leaving Frankie with a sour taste in his mouth and a bitter regret that he had ever told David the truth. Guess he should be grateful David hadn't just slugged him and spit in his face.

But there was nothing he could do about David now. So he said to Pete, "We'll get through the training. We won't end up in the infantry, stuck in the mud in a trench somewhere."

"Promise?" Pete gave him a smile, those blue eyes crinkling in the corners.

Frankie nodded, taking in his fill of that smile. He only realized he was staring when Pete's expression grew puzzled. "What is it?"

Frankie cleared his throat and looked away. "Nothing." Shit. He could *not* develop a crush on Pete. There was no way that would end well.

Pete shrugged, stubbed out his cigarette, and flopped back down. "I'm going to rest while I can, seeing as it's probably the last time we'll get some peace and quiet before we have a sergeant breathing down our necks and yelling for us to march faster."

"You call this peace and quiet?" Frankie said, staring around at the chaos of men jostling for spaces in the barracks and stowing their gear.

"In two days' time, when we're toiling in the hot sun, this will look like paradise," Pete said, covering his eyes with an arm.

CHAPTER TWO

PETE WAS right. Frankie admitted this as he heaved in a breath and forced his legs to keep moving. Twelve fucking miles. Calisthenics at 6:00 a.m. and then marching twelve fucking miles. And that was after they were woken up at 3:00 a.m. when the guys in the class above them dumped buckets of ice water on their heads. Frankie had startled awake with a yell, gotten tangled in the blankets, and fallen out of his bunk, narrowly avoiding being trampled in the general uproar. There had been no sleep after that, of course. At least there had been coffee at breakfast. Tasted awful, but you still got a caffeine boost.

They'd been training for only five days, but it felt like a lot longer. Frankie was adjusting to the rhythms of military life, although he still wasn't saluting sharp enough or making his bed neat enough to suit Sergeant Pascow. He'd gotten a demerit yesterday and had to spend the evening marching it off with a parachute strapped to his back.

Frankie glanced at Pete, who was toiling next to him with his head down and shirt damp with sweat.

"Almost there," Frankie panted, and Pete managed a grin.

"I think I have a blister on every toe."

"You should talk." Frankie slapped Pete's arm. "You're what, ninety percent muscle?" Pete had a heavy build, with thick arms and powerful legs. Frankie had caught himself staring at Pete's ass that morning when he was bending over to make his bed. And in the showers—well, Frankie always turned his back on Pete and made sure he kept the water kind of cold. Every time he started admiring Pete, he told himself he was a damn fool, but he couldn't seem to help it. Pete was kind and didn't treat Frankie like a kid, even though he was three years older. You needed a friend, someone to

10

sit with at meals, commiserate with over hard-ass sergeants, and share news of home every time the mail arrived. Pete and he were becoming good buddies, and if Frankie was beginning to wish they could be more than that, well, hopefully the feeling would pass. He made sure to take a good long look at Betty's photo on the wall every morning to remind himself nothing was coming of this. He just prayed Pete never realized how he felt. It would kill him to see Pete's smile turn to a look of disgust and rejection, like David's had.

As they drew near the base, a PT-17 rumbled by overhead, the yellow fabric covering its frame bright against the blue sky. It dipped alarmingly to the right and then straightened out with a shaky waggle of wings.

Frankie winced. "I bet he's getting an earful from his instructor right about now."

"No wonder they call them the 'yellow peril.'" Pete shook his head. "A little closer and he'd have been belly-up on the ground. Bet you my first flight will be worse than that."

"You'll do fine," Frankie said and then had to shut up as the sergeant came over and yelled at them for talking.

One more week of basic left, and then they'd be transitioning into primary flight training. Half their day would be taken up with ground school, consisting of classes in navigation, aerodynamics, engine mechanics, and other courses. Frankie was dreading this part because it would involve mathematics. He had barely passed his math courses in high school and couldn't imagine he had developed a sudden affinity for it in the past few months.

But the rest of the day would be flight training. He held on to that thought and tried not to think about equations or how much his feet hurt or the letter from his ma with no news from David.

Your brother has started telling his friends you're a pilot. He's becoming quite the expert on aircraft. In other news, the PTA has decided to do a big Thanksgiving dinner to benefit the Red Cross, and of course, I ended up in charge of coordinating who's bringing what dish. The main thing is to make sure

*Mrs. Anderson doesn't bring potato salad because she
always makes it too salty. Oh honey, I can't believe this
will be the first Thanksgiving you won't be with us. I
hope they feed you a decent dinner at the base and
there's plenty of food.*

He was sure his ma was thinking of last year, when he'd eaten
an entire pumpkin pie by himself. June had caught him with the
empty pie plate and made him confess. He had to laugh about Colin,
though. In his next letter, he'd be sure to tell his brother he wasn't a
pilot yet. They didn't pin the wings on you until you'd made it
through advanced training, and that was months away. Not that he
wasn't already imagining how he'd look in the uniform, but there
was no sense in jinxing it.

He always felt a pang of homesickness when he got a letter
from his mother, but they were so busy he didn't have time to
dwell on it. That afternoon they learned how to assemble and
disassemble an M1 carbine and clean all the parts, followed by
some target practice. Roy and George were using the targets next
to Frankie and Pete. He had hoped never to see Roy again after
their first introduction. But their first night on base, Pete had
gotten into an arm wrestling match with Roy and the two had
become friends, much to Frankie's chagrin. He'd warmed up to
Roy a bit since then. Roy had a good sense of humor and a taste
for reckless living to which Frankie could relate. Still, it was hard
to completely shrug off their first meeting and the knowledge of
what Roy would think of him if he ever found out Frankie's
secret. Where Roy went, so did George. He and Roy had bonded
over a shared love of football. Although Roy followed the
Chicago Bears and George followed the Detroit Lions, which had
led to many a heated argument over who had the best quarterback
and defensive line.

The four of them had also gotten acquainted with an older man
named Ed, who was quiet and serious—a nice antidote to Roy and
George. At the moment, Ed, forehead creased in concentration, was
staring down the barrel of his rifle at the target. Pete had already

finished shooting, coming pretty close to the bull's-eye for the most part. Frankie wasn't a bad shot, if he said so himself, and Roy had hit somewhere in the vicinity of the target at least. George blew them all out of the water, hitting the target dead center all but once. Now Ed squeezed off his last few rounds.

Roy whistled. "Damn, Ed. I hope I never have you at my back. You're as liable to hit me as the Jerry."

Ed surveyed his rifle, mouth turned down.

"It'll be different in a plane," Pete assured him.

"Yeah," Frankie muttered. "You'll be *moving*."

Pete gave him a light punch on the arm while the others laughed. Even Ed gave a rueful grin after a moment.

The mail came late that afternoon, and over supper everyone pored over letters or shared copies of *The Stars and Stripes*, the Army's special newspaper for its troops. News about a sea battle in the Pacific near the Solomon Islands dominated the headlines: "Two Japanese ships sunk, hundreds dead. US Navy sustains only light losses."

"Good news?" Frankie asked Pete, who was smiling as he read a letter.

"Nothing special. Just a few lines from Betty. She and her little sister decided to start a victory garden in the spring, and they're deciding on all the stuff they want to plant."

George grabbed the salt shaker by Pete's elbow. "Girlfriends keeping the home fires burning are all well and good, but I hope you're still intending to enjoy yourself to the full."

"Imagine if we ever get to Paris," Roy added. "You know what French girls are like."

Pete gave him a skeptical look. "I'd think they'd have more sense than to fall for idiots like you."

"Hey, all those lectures the Army makes us listen to about VD, I figure there's gotta be someone out there willing to *give* it to us," Roy replied, laughing.

Later that night, when they were lying in their bunks, Pete quietly asked Frankie, "Do you think it's silly to be committed to someone?"

Frankie shifted, wincing at the pull of his sore muscles. "Nah. Roy just thinks with his dick too much. I think it's—" He paused and then made himself say it. "—really beautiful you have someone who loves you and wants to wait for you."

"Thanks, Frankie. Sometimes it seems... I don't know, kind of unfair to her. If I get killed, she'll be stuck with mourning me and all the heartbreak that goes along with it."

"I don't think women go into mourning for years and wear black all the time anymore," Frankie pointed out. "She'll get over you and find some guy who's twice as handsome."

Pete chuckled. "I suppose."

"And I think she'd rather have that connection to you, for always, even if it might not turn out. Although I don't think you'll die, Pete."

"Everybody thinks that, though, don't they? You're always going to be the one who makes it through. But the odds can be pretty stacked against you."

Frankie stayed silent for a few minutes before he spoke again. "You know what really scares me? It's not dying. It's the thought of losing my legs or my arms or something. I don't know what I'd do then. I'd just end up a burden on my parents or my sisters. I wouldn't—" He stopped, the idea weighing down his chest with dread. He'd always been very physical, playing sports, riding horses, climbing trees, running around the house and driving his ma to distraction. If he lost that ability, if he had to rely on someone else to always help him, if he had to just sit and watch—he thought he might go crazy.

"Hey. Hey, it's all right," Pete said softly. "All of us are scared of that too."

Frankie pulled in a deep breath. "Guess it's just best not to think about it and go do what we have to do."

SOME PEOPLE, when they got nervous, couldn't eat. Not Frankie. He just seemed to get hungrier. So on the morning of their first flight—albeit with their instructor doing all of the flying—he ate an extra bowl of oatmeal and three helpings of bacon. Pete watched as he dug in his spoon.

"You sure about that, Frankie?" he asked, fiddling with the lone piece of toast on his plate.

"I'm not going to throw up," Frankie replied around a mouthful. "And neither are you. Stop worrying." He swigged a last mouthful of coffee. "It's going to be swell, you'll see."

"It's too early for this level of enthusiasm," Roy groaned, head propped up on his arm. Roy always seemed to be involved in late-night shenanigans, be it poker games or pranks, and was always the last out of his bed in the morning. "He's like a Labrador getting ready to chase a ball."

"Leave him be, Roy," Pete said. "He's gonna put us all to shame in that cockpit, I bet."

Frankie shrugged, trying not to look too pleased at Pete's words. "I don't know about that."

"I'm sure." Pete grinned. "You're gonna be an ace, Frankie. I know it."

Captain Hollen, his flight instructor, appeared far less sanguine. He gave Frankie a skeptical once-over and then sighed, gesturing for Frankie to follow him to the plane. "I don't want you touching anything without my orders, got it? You're just watching and listening today."

"Yes, sir." Frankie put a hand on the side of the PT-17 they'd be flying, taking a moment to feel its sturdy body under his fingers. Then he scrambled into the cockpit, fit on his helmet, and got strapped in.

"Now watch my movements and stay alert," Hollen said, his voice coming clearly through Frankie's helmet. "You're not here to admire the scenery, got it?"

"Yes, sir," Frankie said again and then remembered Hollen couldn't hear him because the gosport only went one way. The hollow tube hung on Frankie's helmet, the other end extending into the front seat of the cockpit where Hollen could yell instructions into a cone. Whatever questions Frankie might have would have to wait until they were back on the ground.

So now he watched and listened as Hollen checked the mags and then released the brakes and eased the throttle forward. The plane rattled over the runway, the smell of gasoline strong in the air. "Make sure the tower gives you the green light," Hollen said.

With a little bounce, the PT-17 took to the air. Frankie's stomach swooped, and then he forgot everything except the vibrating plane around him and Hollen's voice in his ear.

"Most important thing is to keep your head out of the cockpit and be on the lookout for other aircraft," Hollen told him. "Never lose an awareness of your surroundings."

Frankie nodded, unable to keep from looking over the side and marveling at the rapidly diminishing size of the trucks and buildings on the ground below.

"Now I'm going to show you how to coordinate the rudder and the stick, all right? Pay attention."

At the very end of the flight, Hollen let Frankie take the stick for a few glorious seconds. They were just flying straight, but he was doing it—he was *flying*. He let out a whoop.

"This isn't a joyride!" Hollen snapped, but when they had landed, he clapped Frankie on the shoulder.

"Tomorrow the real work begins," he said, and Frankie nodded, grinning.

He didn't get a chance to see Pete until dinner. Pete's first flight had been after Frankie's, and Frankie was anxious to hear how it had gone.

Pete was poking at the lumpy pile of mashed potatoes on his plate when Frankie slid onto the seat next to him. "You look chipper," Pete observed, smiling a little.

"And you don't," Frankie replied.

Pete shrugged. "It could have been better."

"Did you throw up?"

"No. Wanted to a few times."

"My stomach was jittery at first too."

Pete gave him a skeptical look and then took a bite of his food. "It was a lot to take in," he said after he swallowed. "I'm not sure I can remember it all."

"Yeah, but you don't have to right away. That's why the instructor is there, yelling in your ear."

"You have Hollen too?"

"Yep. He seems a pretty good sort, though. Tough but not a total bastard."

Roy appeared at that juncture, lowering himself with a sigh. "I just saw old Henry Clark hauling a bucket of soap and water out to his plane," he said. "Bet you two bits he washes out by the end of the week."

No one took him up on it. Henry had been an even bigger bundle of nerves than Pete.

"I was just glad to be sitting down," Roy continued, "and not dragging my ass over that blamed obstacle course or doing push-ups."

Pete sighed and pushed away his plate. "Up for a card game, Frankie?" he asked. "I just want to put today behind me."

"Sure." Frankie hopped up, trying not to feel too pleased Pete had asked him.

THAT NIGHT, lying in bed, just on the edge of sleep, he heard Pete's breathing pick up. His sheets rustled, and the cot squeaked.

Frankie swallowed, his cock thickening. No guesses needed as to what Pete was doing. Frankie's mind unhelpfully supplied an image of Pete in the showers, his broad back flexing as he washed his hair.

Inching a hand under the blanket, Frankie squeezed his cock. He rubbed the thin cotton of his shorts against the head, relishing the friction. *Want me to help you with that, Pete?*

He winced. God, he'd sound like a complete idiot. But still… he wondered what Pete would do if he crouched down next to him and whispered it. Pete, with that snapshot of his girlfriend hanging right over his cot.

Pete quieted down a minute or two later. Frankie was left trying to muffle his own sounds as he pumped his cock and came in a sticky mess in his fist.

He felt awkward the next morning, but Pete didn't give any sign he had heard Frankie the night before or been aware that Frankie had been listening to him. As Sergeant Pascow yelled at them to pick up the pace, that he wanted to see them kissing the ground as they did those push-ups, Frankie swore to himself it wouldn't happen again. He should be satisfied—he *was* satisfied—with Pete's friendship. Anything else, well, he had always figured he would never be able to have that. There was no reason why he should be proved wrong.

CHAPTER THREE

IN THE rare downtime they had, Frankie liked to go to the rec room and play Ping-Pong. Roy took him up on a game, unable to turn down a challenge, and when Frankie beat him, Roy started putting others up to it and raking in cash on bets. Frankie made him put it in a common fund for the five of them to use for buying real food the next time they got a pass to leave the base and go into town. Real food like steak dinners or barbecue ribs. Ed, who always bemoaned the awful meals they got, actually went a little misty-eyed thinking about it.

"With your height, I'd have thought you would be a basketball player," Pete said one day after watching Frankie pummel a guy from the class above them.

"My dad and I always used to play Ping-Pong on Saturday nights in the barn," Frankie said. He had played basketball too. He and David had played on the high school team together. Thinking of those times made his gut churn with a combination of anger and sorrow. He'd been so sure David would be supportive and understanding, but apparently even eleven years as friends wasn't long enough to completely know someone.

"I was a football man, myself," Pete said. "Now, what do you say to some studying? Hansen spent half the class yelling at you yesterday."

"You're cruel," Frankie groaned, but let Pete drag him off to practice visual recognition of various aircraft. Pete had been helping him almost every night, whether it was Morse code or navigation.

"I owe you for this," Frankie told him. "Big time." He wanted to add, *I'll do anything you want,* but if Pete realized what he actually meant by that—well, Frankie couldn't take the risk.

19

"Hey, Frankie, what's this one?"

Frankie snapped back to the present and frowned at the aircraft silhouette on the card Pete held. "Um, a Spitfire?"

"Nope, a Hurricane."

"Hey, they're both on our side. I know they're friendly."

Pete gave him a look and held up another card.

"Oh, now that one I know." Frankie grinned. "P-51 Mustang. The best aircraft in the skies."

Pete flipped the card around to look at it. "It can go up to 437 miles per hour." He whistled. "Can't quite imagine what that'll feel like."

"It'll feel swell." Frankie leaned back in his chair. "You'll be here and then gone the next minute." He snapped his fingers. "Like that. And don't say you think you can't handle it because you can."

"Maybe. I did another ground loop today when I landed. Went right off the runway and my plane turned in a circle, wing dragging. And that was after I forgot to check my mags before take-off. Hollen yelled at me for a good ten minutes after it was over."

"He yelled at me, too, for pulling out of a dive too late. He thought I was gonna crash straight into the ground."

"'Cause you're a crazy bastard, trying to do a split-S in a PT-17, for Christ's sake." Pete leaned over and punched Frankie's shoulder lightly. "If you don't slow it down, you'll never make it overseas."

Pete was probably right, but Frankie couldn't help wanting to go fast, to push his plane to its utmost limits.

THANKSGIVING DINNER at the base was adequate, but Frankie spent the entire evening fantasizing over memories of his ma's sweet potatoes and watermelon pickles. A week later, having breakfast under the too-bright lights in the mess hall, given the sun didn't rise until later by this time in December, Roy watched as Frankie shoveled fried potatoes into his mouth. "Don't tell me, you're soloing today."

Frankie nodded, mouth too full to speak. He'd had ten hours in the cockpit, and now it was time to prove he could cut it by himself.

"Slow down, don't choke," Pete said, squeezing his shoulder as he sat down beside him. "Besides, you don't need to be nervous. You'll do fine."

"It's not so bad," George put in. He had survived his first solo flight yesterday and could adopt an air of calm superiority.

Frankie could have reminded him that he had missed his landing twice, but he didn't. He might make the same mistake or worse. He had felt pretty confident up until last night and then had lain awake imagining a litany of things that could go wrong.

He stayed nervous through the preflight check, and his heartbeat inched upward when the engine started. As he taxied down the runway, he was painfully conscious of his solitude and the fact that if something did go wrong, it was up to him to fix it. But as he picked up speed, he started to feel more settled. When the plane left the ground with a hop, the tension eased, replaced by excitement.

Hollen's voice crackled over the radio. "Remember, Norris, just take her up and around the block. Nothing fancy."

"Yes, sir," Frankie replied, trying to suppress a grin. Nothing fancy—but surely it wouldn't hurt to do one little roll, once he was safely out of sight of the tower. Hollen had demonstrated it the other day, and Frankie had been itching to try it.

The plane sped up as he pushed the throttle forward. The frame started vibrating at a new pitch, and the engine made an unhappy sort of noise, but Frankie kept pushing it. Just a little farther, a little faster. Holding his breath, he turned the stick sharply. Half a second later, the plane was on its back and the only thing holding him into the open cockpit was his shoulder straps. Another flip of the stick had him upright again.

Frankie sucked in a breath and then expelled it with a giddy laugh. *Gee, that was fun!* He decided nothing was ever going to keep him from flying, not when this untethered joy waited for him up in the air.

21

He wanted to do a roll again, immediately, but the clock was ticking. So he made himself turn around and focus on keeping the little ball on the instrument panel centered.

The next trick was landing. Hollen always said it was one of the hardest parts of flying, and he told Frankie not to be ashamed if he overshot and had to do the approach again. But Frankie wanted to put paid to the smug smile on George's face. He wanted the perfect flight.

"Green Three requesting permission to land," he radioed in as he approached.

"All clear, Green Three," the operator returned.

It wasn't until he started to drop down to the landing strip that he realized he was going too fast. He tried to throttle back, but he still hit the ground at a high speed. Gritting his teeth, he braked hard, the stick fighting against his grip, trying to veer off to the side.

And then suddenly everything was still. Blinking, he released his death grip on the controls and sank back into his seat. Damn. Nothing like a little adrenaline rush at the end.

"What goddamn race were you running, Norris?" Hollen demanded, jogging up to him as Frankie unbuckled his straps and hopped out. "You never come in so fast on a landing, you hear me?"

"Yes, sir," Frankie said. "Sorry, sir."

Hollen gave him a suspicious look, as though he suspected Frankie had been trying a few unauthorized tricks. But he said, "Well, besides that hiccup at the end, I'd say you're cleared for solo flying from here on out."

Frankie grinned. "Thanks, sir!" Hollen shook his head but dismissed him, and Frankie ran off to find Pete.

Pete was in their barracks, changing into his flight suit. Frankie dashed over and flung an arm around his neck, pulling him into a half-hug.

"It went swell!" he said. "I did this roll, Pete, hanging upside down, and then I came in too fast, but I pulled it off, and—"

Pete detached him gently, laughing at Frankie's enthusiastic chatter. He gave him a congratulatory shake before letting go. "Knew you'd do great."

Frankie flushed, smiling. He wanted so badly to lean against Pete again. If Pete would put his arms around him, giving him a kiss just to the side of his ear, breath ruffling Frankie's hair....

He shut his eyes for a second, getting a hold of himself. "We should do something to celebrate," he said when he opened them again, proud his voice sounded normal. "Once you pass your flight."

"If I do," Pete returned.

"You will." Frankie's fingers snuck out and tugged the lapel of Pete's shirt straight before he could stop them.

"Thanks for the vote of confidence."

"We'll get Roy, George, and Ed together—maybe go blow all my Ping-Pong winnings on some fancy steak dinner." He'd rather it was just the two of them, but it would sound too weird to say so.

Frankie trailed after Pete back to the field. "Good luck," he said, as Pete went toward his plane. Pete gave him a halfhearted thumbs up.

Ed came over and joined him a minute later. "Heard you passed your solo. Well done."

"Thanks." Frankie frowned, watching as Pete's plane began to move shakily forward.

"That Pete out there?" Ed asked, and when Frankie nodded, he said, "I should have known. You follow him around like a puppy."

"I do not!" Frankie replied, stung and scared. It would be bad enough to be teased for acting like a wet-behind-the-ears kid. He couldn't afford anyone realizing his feelings went far beyond simple admiration. Ed chuckled. "It's okay, Norris. Pete's a good friend. A real solid guy. Better than those two ne'er-do-wells, Roy and George."

"I get that you're older, but I'm not dumb, okay?" Frankie retorted, resentful of Ed's condescension and still nervous.

"All right." Ed held up a placating hand. "I'm just saying."

Frankie turned his attention back to Pete. He must be having some kind of trouble or he would have taken off by now. At last, the plane lifted into the air, wobbled around for a few seconds and then started off on a less-than-straight course to the west.

Objectively, Frankie could admit Pete wasn't such a good pilot, but when Ed noted that fact, he jumped to Pete's defense.

"It's only his first solo! He'll get better."

"There's not much time to get better, though, is there?" Ed crossed his arms over his chest and shook his head. "We're already in an accelerated training program. And once we're overseas, well, dogfights aren't the place to practice basic procedures."

"He'll get better," Frankie repeated. "And he'll have me—and the rest of us—to look out for him."

He could feel Ed watching him, and he kept his eyes resolutely on the sky.

"You have a girlfriend, Frankie?" Ed finally asked.

"No," Frankie replied, instantly wary. He figured it was a bigger risk to lie, though, and have to keep a story straight every time someone asked.

"Me either." Ed turned his gaze back on the field. "Don't intend to," he added.

Frankie's breath caught. Was Ed saying what he thought he might be saying?

A smile flickered over Ed's face. "Don't look so scared. But you should come with me to the music room after dinner tonight. I have some friends I think you should meet."

Instinctive caution warred with curiosity as Frankie pondered Ed's offer. Ed might be implying there were more men like him on the base. Frankie could hardly credit it. Just Ed being queer seemed like a lot to believe. He'd never met anyone else. Fooling around with a bunch of guys in the swimming hole when he was thirteen was one thing, even if there had been some mutual hand jobs and cornholing going on. But he was supposed to have gotten over that. The rest of those guys had all gone on to get girlfriends. It had seemed like he was the only one who hadn't been interested. But maybe, just maybe, he hadn't known where to look.

"Okay," Frankie agreed, still wary, but curiosity won out over caution. Ed left a few minutes later, while Frankie stayed to wait for Pete.

Pete wasn't in a particularly good mood when he did get back and barely managed to pull off a rough landing. Frankie tried to coax him into a better humor, but Pete didn't want to be soothed and finally went off to write to Betty. Of course that would cheer him up where Frankie had failed. Trying not to feel jealous, Frankie went to find Ed. He'd been of half a mind not to show up, but he might as well, seeing as how Pete didn't want him around.

Frankie had never been to the music room before because he couldn't sing, and his one attempt at the trumpet in high school had been an abject failure. But as soon as he walked in the door, he started to think that had been a big mistake on his part. Two guys were sitting on the piano stool and one of them actually had his arm around the other's shoulders and was leaning into him, smiling. Another group was seated around a table, laughing and smoking. One guy was fluttering his hands and saying, "But girls, you won't believe the rough I pulled on the weekend." He broke off, raising his eyebrows. "Why, Edward, who is this handsome stranger?"

"This is Frankie," Ed replied. "Frankie, this is Tom. Of course we usually call him Dolly, as he's a Dolly Dancer—sits in the office all day and writes memos for the CO and types up letters." Tom—Dolly—blew him a little kiss, and Frankie flushed. He'd never met someone so swishy, never mind that he was behaving like this in the middle of an Army base.

Ed was continuing with the introductions. "Jack's to his right and Junior on his left. Michael and Robert are over there by the piano." Jack, sprawled in the chair, gave Frankie a lazy nod. Junior, whose pale skin was flaking from sunburn despite the fact that it was December, smiled. He couldn't be much more than eighteen either, but he looked more relaxed and confident than Frankie felt, that was for sure. Robert and Michael gave brief waves and then went back to their music.

Frankie managed a hoarse hello. Ed started to lead the way to the table to join the others, but Frankie grabbed his arm. "How did

25

you know?" he asked, keeping his voice low. "How did you know I was... queer?" He stumbled over it, only the second time in his life he'd said it aloud.

Ed gave him a smile, kind of tired but sympathetic. "The way you stare at Pete? Having been there myself a few times, I know what it looks like."

"Oh." Frankie jammed his hands in his pockets and rocked on his heels. He flicked another nervous glance at the other guys.

"Nobody here will say anything to anyone else," Ed assured him. "And if you want to leave, that's fine too."

He didn't want to leave, though. A thousand questions were popping into his head, for one thing.

"No, I'll stay," he said, and he took the chair Junior pushed out for him.

"Michael, for God's sake, will you play something more cheerful?" Jack said.

The melancholy strains of "You'll Never Know" stopped abruptly.

"Fuck off, Jack," Robert said, tightening his arm around Michael's shoulders. "You know Benny just got shipped to the Pacific."

"I told him he shouldn't set his heart on a sailor," Dolly put in. "Although Lord knows, they're hard to avoid. We went into San Diego two weeks ago, and I was *tripping* over yeomen."

"You'll find a new guy next weekend," Jack said dismissively.

"Just because you'll fuck anything that moves...," Michael began.

Junior put his hand on Frankie's arm, scooting his chair closer. "Ignore them. They'll be at it for a while. So where are you from?"

"Idaho. You?"

"Northern California—Oakland. Spent most of my time in San Francisco, though." Junior glanced at Ed. "I take it he doesn't know much, huh?"

"I think drag balls and Turkish baths are pretty thin on the ground in Idaho," Ed replied. "Am I right, Frankie?"

Frankie nodded, embarrassed.

"But all those cowboys." Junior grinned. "Didn't you ever…?"

"No," Frankie muttered.

"Well, don't worry about it," Junior advised. "We'll get you a little something."

The piano started up again—resolutely wistful. Jack rolled his eyes and stubbed out his cigarette.

The talk went on for a few minutes, and Frankie started to relax. Finally he blurted out, "But aren't you afraid someone will catch you here?"

Junior laughed. "It's just a bunch of guys enjoying some R and R. No different from everyone else."

"And that," Dolly said, "is the beauty of the Army. You will never find a better selection of roughs and queers all in one place. Facilities provided by the government too."

"But if the wrong person discovered this…." Frankie trailed off, confused, unable to imagine being so *open.*

"We know the risks," Ed said quietly. "But sometimes you have to take risks. The COs here don't seem interested in pursuing any kind of investigations. Of course, it isn't like that everywhere. But you get to know which places are safer than others."

As Frankie and Ed walked back to their barracks a while later, Frankie said quietly, "I guess I've just been stupid, not noticing you or Junior or… well, that I'm not the only one."

Ed shrugged. "We try not to draw attention, most of us, that is. Dolly always puts on a bit of a show, and Junior isn't exactly subtle. But Jack, he propositioned the wrong guy once and got the shit beaten out of him. As for myself, I…." He paused, as though considering how to phrase it. "It was hard for me to lie about it in order to get accepted into the Air Forces. But it's bullshit, that I shouldn't be able to serve my country." He shot Frankie a rueful smile. "Not that I'm saying you should go shove it in Roy's or George's or Pete's face or anything. No point in asking for trouble."

27

Frankie nodded. "Do you think Pete guesses?" he couldn't help asking.

Ed's eyes softened. "No, I don't think so. But you know you don't have a chance there, right?"

"I know." He just wished he could make his heart believe it.

CHAPTER FOUR

THE PT-17 shuddered beneath him as Frankie pushed the throttle to the limit. He spared one hand to tuck his scarf more tightly around his neck. It protected his skin from chafing under his helmet and also kept him warmer. December in California was nothing like December in Idaho, but at high altitudes, the wind got chilly no matter what. It sure was strange to look down and see green fields, though, instead of snow. It had rained all day yesterday, and even though he knew it was almost Christmas, it seemed more like summer to him. Usually at this time of year, he would be shoveling three-foot drifts of snow off the back porch. He kind of liked being able to go outside in nothing but a light jacket, absent the usual winter paraphernalia of a heavy coat, gloves, hat, and boots.

Imagine if he got sent to the Pacific to fight the Japs. It would be hot and humid, a tropical sun blazing down. Or maybe it would be North Africa, just as hot but desert dry, flying missions into Italy to support the invasion. The steady advancement of the Allies since September had been halted just above Naples, the Nazis digging in behind the Winter Line and holding fast. And of course, he could always get sent to Europe. Surely soon the Allies would be launching an invasion of France and Germany. They couldn't just let Hitler sit there, building all the planes and bombs and tanks he needed.

Glancing out the canopy, he took note of the landmarks below. He recognized the white barn—he'd have to head to the north a little and circle back around to the base. So far he hadn't gotten lost. Roy had managed to lose his way one day and had to depend on instructions from the radio tower to guide him back. As Frankie turned in a half-circle, he spotted a herd of cows, placidly

29

grazing. Surely it wouldn't hurt to give them a bit of excitement in their day.

His plane buzzed about ten yards over their heads. Looking back, he saw the herd scatter, tails waving madly as they dashed in all directions. He turned around just in time to swoop up and over a patch of oak trees, letting out a shout and grinning. Boy, he couldn't wait to advance to basic training where he'd get to fly a BT-13, a Vultee Vibrator that had a slight edge on the PT-17 in terms of speed. And then he'd make it to advanced training and the AT-6 before finally, *finally* getting to the real thing, the P-51 Mustang. He'd seen two flying over just the other day, in fact, and had stared after them like some awestruck kid. To think he'd get to fly one of them soon. He knew he shouldn't count his chickens before they hatched, as his mother would say, but he had been made to do this, to be up here, gravity and the slowness of the earth a distant memory.

When he finally landed, windswept and hungry as a horse, Lieutenant Hollen was waiting for him, looking grim. Frankie's smile faltered, and he tried to smooth down his hair, which was sticking up every which way thanks to his helmet.

"Good flight, Norris?"

"Uh, yes, sir."

Hollen raised his eyebrows. "Anything you want to tell me?"

Frankie swallowed. "Um, no?"

"Then do you want to explain to me why we received a call from an irate farmer who witnessed one of our planes spooking his cattle herd? You were the only one out in that area this morning, Norris."

Frankie's stomach sank, and he tried a sheepish grin. Hollen's frown didn't waver. "Sorry, sir. I just thought I would, um, practice flying a little closer to the ground. I didn't see the cows until it was too late."

"Do you know how many times I've heard that excuse?" Hollen pointed back to the base. "Hope you didn't have any other plans this afternoon, because you're going to spend all of it walking off demerits."

"Yes, sir." Frankie bit back a sigh.

"And, Norris? Remember, this is serious. We're fighting a war, and we don't have the time for stupid pranks. I don't want to hear about this sort of thing from you again."

"Yes, sir." That sobered him up more than the demerits. It was true—he hadn't joined the Air Forces for kicks. He was here to do a job, and he should buckle down and do it right.

Pete approved of this attitude when Frankie stumbled back to the barracks that evening, shoulders aching from lugging his parachute around, legs sore from marching, and told him what had happened.

"It's more than just making our families proud of us," Pete said, looking up from sewing a new button on his shirt. "We have a responsibility to our country and to everyone who's suffering in this war." He sighed. "I just wish I had a better chance of meeting that responsibility."

"Come on, Pete. You're going to advance to basic flight training with the rest of us. You've improved a lot." Wincing, Frankie pulled off his boots and socks, wiggling his toes.

Pete gave him a look. "I've never stuck a clean landing, Frankie. And I still can't get that damn ball centered on the turn-and-bank indicator."

"But we still have months of training to go. It'll be spring or summer before they make us pilots. By that time—"

"Give it a rest." Pete snipped off the thread, his voice sharp. Then he sighed. "Not that I don't appreciate your optimism, Frankie, but it can only take a guy so far."

"Sorry," he muttered, guilt swamping him. His encouragement was due in large part to his own reluctance to face the fact that Pete might leave. He didn't want to be alone. Oh, Ed, Roy, and George would probably still be there, but he wasn't close to them, not like he was to Pete. Of course, he couldn't tell Pete everything. His experience with David had taught him that. Part of him thought he must be a masochist, wanting Pete to stay, his presence always a tantalizing reminder of what Frankie could never have. But in some ways, that didn't matter. Pete was a good friend, and Frankie would miss him something awful if he washed out of pilot training.

TWO NIGHTS later Frankie, Pete, Roy, Ed, and George all piled into George's Studebaker Champion and drove into Santa Ana to have a pre-Christmas supper. A place called the Paradise Hotel had special offers for servicemen. George had been there once before and could vouch for their steaks. Frankie's mouth was already watering at the thought of real butter for their potatoes and a tender, medium-rare rib eye. As they drove down the street, they passed two empty, boarded-up stores.

"Used to belong to Japs," George said.

In one of the windows, prominently displayed, was an American flag.

Frankie remembered a conversation with Junior one night. Junior had known a Japanese family who owned a grocery store near his neighborhood in Oakland. "When the government made them leave, they asked my parents to look after their dog," he had related. "A real sweetie, some kind of spaniel mix." He wondered if the people who had owned these stores had also had pets and if anyone had volunteered to look after them while they were gone.

They pulled up to the Paradise Hotel a few blocks later. It was decorated with Christmas lights, the big round bulbs throwing colored shadows across the façade. They had barely sat down at their table when George and Roy started flirting with the waitress.

"You remember me?" George asked, giving her a smile. "I was in here a week or so ago. I remember *your* name. Sally, right?"

She blushed. "That's right."

"It's there on her name tag," Roy pointed out.

"Yeah, but I didn't peek. Scout's honor," George protested.

Frankie had to admit Roy was very handsome. George might be more homely, with his red hair and freckles, but he came across as sweeter. He leaned over to Ed and whispered, "Fifty cents says she goes with George."

Ed chuckled, "No sense betting against a sure thing."

Meanwhile, Roy was giving Sally a smile of his own. "I'm going to remember your name too."

Sally laughed and rolled her eyes. "All right, boys, what'll it be?"

They ordered their dinner and drinks. Frankie even asked for a gin and tonic, and Sally didn't blink an eye. The perks of being in a uniform.

Roy whistled when she had left to place their orders. "Now that's what I'd like to have for dessert."

"Betcha she'd rather have me," George retorted. "By virtue of our longer acquaintance."

"Ed and I agree with George," Frankie said. "Sorry, Roy, but the fates are against you tonight."

"Maybe if you didn't pant after anything in a skirt like a pair of overeager dogs, you'd have a chance of actually winning a solid girl," Pete added.

Roy and George looked unimpressed.

"Hey, we get you're a one girl kind of guy," Roy told him, "but that doesn't have to stop the rest of us from enjoying ourselves. Although Ed is too old and Frankie is too shy."

"Thanks," Ed said dryly.

Frankie let it stand. Better to be thought too shy than the other alternatives. Then he caught Ed giving him a smile, and he returned it, smothering a laugh. Sure felt nice to have someone to laugh with about moments like this. Although he couldn't help but remember what Ed had told him about keeping a low profile and compare that to how Roy and George could hit on any woman within a fifty-foot radius.

The talk turned then to flying, a debate on whether it would be better to face a German Me 109 or a Jap Zero, and then to the war in general.

"My cousin is a radio operator with the Tenth Light Division," George said. "They're stuck somewhere in Italy. He doesn't think they'll make any progress until the spring."

"Do you think we'll keep going through Italy?" Frankie asked. "Or try for France?"

Pete shrugged. "The Nazis have got the entire French coast fortified. They expect an attack from Britain."

"Yeah, but they can't defend every inch of it," Roy protested. "Some spots are weaker than others."

"Stalin will keep pressuring until we open a second front," Ed said. "We have to do it sometime. Probably right when we arrive, fresh from training."

Sally returned with their drinks at this juncture. Roy and George each made another borderline-inappropriate comment. Sally ignored both of them.

George stared wistfully at her retreating figure and then tossed back a shot of bourbon. He leaned forward. "I think we should finish Hitler off quick so we can concentrate on the Japs. They're the ones who attacked us, after all."

"So far it hasn't been all that quick." Ed shook his head. "Berlin will be a real tough nut to crack. And if we don't watch out, the Soviets will swoop in and take it all for themselves."

Frankie had to admit he didn't keep up with all the political back and forth between the Allies. "Just point me in the right direction and tell me what to shoot," he said aloud.

"That's the attitude to have," George said approvingly. He raised his glass. "To our first mission and blowing the hell out of the enemy."

BACK IN the car after dinner, Frankie rested his head on the seat back and regarded the dimly lighted street, which was swaying dizzily in his vision. He shouldn't have had that third drink. His ma didn't approve of alcohol, and he had only tasted some beers and the odd shot of liquor before enlisting.

"That was a damn good steak," Pete said, stretching his legs out next to Frankie's. Ed was in the front seat, all three of them waiting for Roy and George to finish sweet-talking Sally.

Frankie nodded, eyes caught on the small smile just tilting Pete's mouth upward. The top two buttons on his shirt were open, his sleeves rolled up.

"It's been a great night," Frankie agreed, stumbling a little over the words, wanting to put his thumb just there, on the dip in Pete's collarbone. He'd *definitely* had too much to drink.

"I had a letter from Betty today," Pete continued.

"Oh." Frankie looked away, staring out the windshield at the blinking "vacancy" sign on a motel across the street.

"She says I should listen to you and not worry so much about my flying."

It took Frankie a minute to work through that. "You told her about me?"

"Sure. You're my crazy friend from Idaho." Pete smiled at him. "We survived Sergeant Pascow and his never-ending marches together. I'm pretty sure that means we're bonded for life."

Frankie hiccupped, horrified to find tears threatening to rise. He couldn't help wanting more than Pete could give him. Solemnly, he put his hand over his heart. "I'll feel it right here if anything ever happens to you."

Ed snorted in the front seat, and Pete rolled his eyes. "You had one too many drinks, I think," he said. "Just try not to throw up on my shoes on the way home, okay?"

"Okay," Frankie agreed. "Did you really tell your girlfriend about me?"

"Yes, Frankie," Pete said patiently. "We just got through talking about it."

Ed twisted around to look at them. "Maybe you should be quiet now, Frankie." He raised his eyebrows meaningfully.

Roy and George's arrival silenced whatever other drunken comments he might have made. George was jubilant, Roy downcast. "She agreed to a date on Saturday," George said smugly.

Pete raised his eyebrows. "You know we're only likely to be stationed here a week or two more at most? Then we'll get moved to basic training at another base."

George shrugged. "Neither of us are looking for anything long term."

"How are you going to last it, Pete?" Roy demanded. "Going the whole war without getting any? I mean, being faithful is sweet and all, but, jeez."

"Hey, he's got the wedding night to look forward to," Ed put in.

Pete flushed. "Shut up, would you? I don't want any of your dirty minds even contemplating Betty."

The other three teased Pete all the way back to the base. Frankie sat staring out the window, trying not to throw up and also trying not to think about what Pete would be like in bed.

Pete had to haul him to the barracks. Frankie kicked off his shoes and then rolled into the blankets, too tired and drunk to mess with his clothes.

"There'll be hell to pay in the morning when you try to get the wrinkles out of your uniform," Pete warned him, but Frankie waved him off, burrowing his head in his pillow. He didn't want to talk to Pete anymore tonight. Sometimes it hurt too much, wanting what he could never have nor even acknowledge wanting. He just wanted to sleep. Maybe he would dream about somebody else, like that actor John Garfield, who was equally unobtainable but in a way that didn't hurt. He must have seen *Four Daughters* five times in the theater when it came out, so he ought to have plenty of fuel for the fire.

FRANKIE WOKE with a splitting headache the next morning and no recollection of his dreams. He choked down some toast at breakfast and took grim comfort in the fact that Roy and George looked just as awful as he felt. By afternoon he was feeling better. And on Monday, the real good news came. He'd made it into basic training and was scheduled to report at Marana Army Air Field in Arizona in two weeks. He went straight back to the barracks, whistling.

When Pete came in, Frankie called out a greeting. "Hey! So, I was thinking maybe on the way to Arizona we might find a place to get a decent ice cream soda...." He trailed off, noting Pete's somber face. "What is it?"

Pete sat down on his cot. "I'm not advancing. I washed out."

Frankie stared, shocked. "But...."

"Hollen didn't feel my performance was improving."

"Well, he's an idiot!"

Pete shook his head. "I appreciate it, Frankie, but he's right. I've never been able to master the controls. I'm all over the place, and it would only be a matter of time before I hurt myself, or worse, one of you guys."

"But you can't just give up," Frankie protested.

"I'm not giving up. I'm admitting I'm not suited for being a pilot."

Frankie chewed on this for a moment. "What are you going to do, then?"

"They want me to transfer to navigator school." Pete smiled. "I guess all that studying we did together has paid off."

Frankie nodded slowly. A hollow ache had lodged itself in his chest. He'd known this could happen, but now it was a fact. "Will you... write to me?" he asked carefully, not sure how Pete would take it.

But Pete just kept smiling. "Sure thing."

"Be careful," Frankie added. "As much as you can."

Pete laughed. "I'm pretty sure that should be my line to you. You're the one always pulling crazy stunts. So *you* take care."

"I'll try." He managed a smile. "Maybe I'll see you in Idaho once all this is over."

"Yep, Idaho or hell. One or the other."

Frankie wished he could ask him for a picture. It would be nice to put it up on the wall, like other guys did with their girlfriends' pictures.

He tried to comfort himself with the knowledge it could have been worse. Pete could have died in a training accident. But of course, he could still die. Any of them could. Now they'd just be farther apart when it happened.

CHAPTER FIVE

ED CORNERED him outside the mess hall that night. "I heard Pete's getting transferred."

Frankie shrugged.

Ed heaved a sigh. "This weekend, you're going to come with Dolly, Junior, and I into San Diego. Find something to take your mind off this."

Frankie wanted to protest that Pete was leaving on Saturday, but it was stupid to mope around the base and wave after Pete's bus like a lovesick teenager.

And so Saturday morning found him in a car with Ed and the others. He'd given Pete a hug before he left and once again promised to write. He'd sworn to himself he wouldn't feel too cut up about it. Like Ed said, it was foolish. He was doing all right, laughing along to a story Junior was telling about his comic misadventures with a cop in San Francisco before the war and how when the cop said, "I've got a nine-inch baton here, sonny," it had *not* been innuendo, when the radio started playing Bing Crosby's "My Buddy."

Listening to Crosby sing about missing his buddy, that sudden absence of a familiar voice, and long, lonely nights with his friend gone—well, Frankie was done for after that. Gritting his teeth, he stared out the window, trying to ignore the hollow spot Pete had left behind.

Ed, sitting next to him, noticed. "Ah, Frankie, don't mind it so," he said quietly.

"What is it, sugar?" Dolly asked, glancing at him in the rearview mirror.

"One of the guys in our unit washed out," Ed explained. "Frankie was sweet on him. He was a regular guy, though, not even trade."

Dolly and Junior made sympathetic noises.

"You can't look for love at a time like this," Junior said. "Everyone getting shipped off to places a thousand miles apart. You gotta enjoy the moment." He twisted in his seat to look at Frankie. "You ready for some fun?" he asked, grinning.

"Hell, yes." Frankie let his head thump back on the seat. He shut his eyes. "I really, really am."

THE FUN proved to be a yeoman named Sergio who Junior introduced him to on Mission Beach.

"Frankie's looking for some kicks," Junior said.

"I can do that." Sergio's dark eyes traveled up and down Frankie's body. Maybe he would blame Frankie's subsequent blush on the sun. They had changed out of their uniforms at a "locker" Dolly knew of that, illegally, supplied civilian clothes, just in case any MPs from the local base were out at the cruising spots. Frankie's shirt was tighter than he normally would have worn. But Sergio still had his Navy uniform on, and it was tight in all the right places too. "I have a room at the Y," Sergio added.

"Perfect." Junior slapped Frankie on the back. "I'll leave you to it, then. See you bright and early for the drive back tomorrow, Frankie."

Frankie was left staring at Sergio, unsure how to proceed.

"Shall we?" Sergio asked after a moment, and Frankie lurched into motion, following him through the crowds. Sand leaked into his shoes, but he ignored it. He wondered if he should admit his limited experience with guys to Sergio or just go with it.

"So, you're a pilot," Sergio said.

Frankie nodded. "Yep. Well, I will be, once I get through training." Some of his nervousness slipped away, thinking about being in the cockpit, the engine noise thrumming through him. "And gee, it's swell."

Sergio chuckled. "My father, he was a fisherman in Italy. So I picked the Navy, thinking it was in my blood." Frankie had guessed he must be Italian, with his olive skin, curly dark hair, and slight accent. He hadn't met many Italians. His father always called them "wops." Every time the newspaper carried word of a labor strike, he would say, "Those damned wops are at it again," and his mother would chide him for cursing.

He thought about what his father would say if he knew his son was about to get done by an Italian and felt a little ill.

"And is it? In your blood?" he asked.

Sergio shook his head ruefully. "No. I do not like being squeezed into a ship with hundreds of other men."

"Really?" Frankie grinned. "I wouldn't mind it."

"Well, there is that." Sergio smiled back at him. "But then you are floating on the ocean, and you hear the sound of a plane overhead, and you think 'perhaps this one will drop a bomb on us,' and there is nowhere to go. I cannot run or hide."

Frankie's grin faded. "It's brave of you to keep getting back on the ship, then," he said at last.

Sergio shrugged. "Sometimes I think about trying to get out of it. I've thought of going to the doctor and saying, 'I'm a homosexual,' and getting a blue discharge. But I want to fight, even if I hate the small ships. You know what they do to men like us in Germany?"

Frankie shook his head, guessing it wasn't good.

"They're being killed. I met a man from Germany who got out just before things got really bad, and he knew. I figure no one else will fight for them, and so I must."

Frankie looked at Sergio's calm face and the determination in his eyes and felt a new respect for this man who had admitted his fear but was not going to let it stop him. And for the first time, he was... *proud* of his abnormal nature. What had always been a source of fear and shame suddenly seemed a badge of honor, binding him to men like Sergio or Ed. They protected each other, fought for each other, and proved they were not cowards.

The attendant at the desk of the Y.M.C.A. didn't bat an eye when Sergio and Frankie strolled past.

"He's wise," Sergio said. "Not queer, but wise to us and our ways."

"Our ways?"

Sergio chuckled again. "I was thinking my mouth on you, but I could be persuaded to try something else."

"Um, no objections from me," Frankie stuttered, hoping desperately he didn't come the second Sergio unbuttoned his pants.

He didn't, but it was a near thing.

The memory of that room with its spare furnishings, the framed picture of some palm trees and a lurid sunset on the wall, and the peeling white paint around the windowsill was always going to be etched in his mind. He would always remember Sergio, too, kneeling in front of him, looking up with a smile before he took Frankie's cock in his mouth and sucked gently.

He kind of wanted to cry, because it felt so good and Sergio was being so kind, even though Frankie's inexperience had to be obvious. The fact that he rested his shaking fingers on dark hair instead of blond also made him sad, even though he had tried to shove Pete into the farthest reaches of his mind.

So he closed his eyes instead and just felt. Sergio liked taking it slow. His tongue lapped a long, wet stripe up the underside of Frankie's cock, then played at the head for a while, darting in for quick licks and then retreating, teasing Frankie until he let out a groan of frustration. Sergio's chuckle puffed against him, and then the warmth of his mouth engulfed him again. This time Sergio took him deeper, sliding his tongue up and down as he did.

Frankie made inarticulate noises and pressed his knees against him, trying to hold off the inevitable. Sergio gave his thigh an encouraging rub and sucked harder.

His body curved into a bow when his orgasm hit, and he held on to Sergio's head, fingers woven into his curls as he panted. It seemed to go on forever, his come pulsing in a steady stream.

When at last it released him, he stayed bent over, feeling weak and shaky. Sergio swallowed, wiping at his mouth, and then

41

straightened, still on his knees but tall enough to rest his head against Frankie's sternum. He wrapped his arms around Frankie, holding him while his trembling eased. Frankie laid his cheek against Sergio's curly hair.

They didn't talk, but after a bit Sergio started undoing the buttons of Frankie's shirt and easing it off him. The rest of their clothes followed until they were stretched out naked on the sheets, arms curved together, and Sergio's cock slippery and hard against Frankie's stomach.

"What do you want?" Frankie whispered. He didn't know if he could manage a blow job. He felt so strange—a little sleepy, definitely happy, and yet somehow brittle and breakable.

"Take me in your hand," Sergio whispered back. Frankie did, and Sergio wrapped his own hand over Frankie's, guiding him, showing him what he liked. He hooked a leg over Frankie's thigh, getting closer, the dark hair on his chest and stomach scratchy against Frankie's pale skin.

When Sergio brushed his lips over Frankie's, Frankie hesitated a moment and then nodded, opening up under the tender questing of his tongue. His hand learned the shape of Sergio's cock, and when he came, the sticky heat dripped over his fingers, smearing on his stomach.

They slept, waking up an hour or so later to share a bottle of Coke and some potato chips. Then they dozed, gave each other hand jobs when they both got hard again, and finally Frankie fell asleep to the muted sound of a radio a few doors down and Sergio's light snores.

He woke in the morning to Sergio shaking his shoulder. Frankie rolled onto his back, blinking.

"What time is it?"

"Almost eight."

"Dang." Frankie sat up and yawned. "I have to meet the guys in half an hour."

"Better get dressed, then." Sergio ruffled his hair. "You can borrow a towel."

Soaping himself up in the shower, Frankie remembered Sergio's hands on his body, tracing the path they had taken with his own. He took a deep breath and let it out, the water hot against his shoulders and back. His first night with another guy. Maybe he had thought it would change him in some way. He didn't feel that different from usual, though. He still wanted eggs for breakfast, still couldn't wait to go flying, and still wanted to see the latest Bogart film. But now he had this memory of someone taking care of him, holding him, kissing him. Now that it had happened once, he knew it wasn't impossible, and it could happen again.

He said good-bye to Sergio in the lobby.

"Thanks," Frankie said, suddenly and inexplicably shy. "I had a great time."

"It was my pleasure." Sergio smiled. "*Buon viaggio.*"

"*Buon viaggio,*" Frankie replied, mangling the phrase horribly. He hesitated, wishing there was more he could say, but Sergio gave him a gentle push toward the door.

"Feel any better?" Ed asked him when they were back in the car. He looked tired but satisfied, and Dolly was fast asleep in the back seat. Only Junior was whistling perkily.

Frankie thought for a moment and then nodded. "I think so. I'm still going to miss Pete, though."

Ed swung the car onto the highway, pushing down on the accelerator. "I know." He glanced at Frankie and smiled. "But just remember, you're not alone in this."

Not alone. Frankie rolled those words in his mind. He'd never imagined, back in Idaho, that this whole world existed, that there were others—lots of others—like him. He'd always thought if he met others who shared his abnormal nature, it would be in the locked ward of a psych hospital. It was such a relief to find out he'd been wrong.

CHAPTER SIX

THE BASE in Arizona was even farther from, as Roy put it, "tits and telephones." The small town of Marana was nearby but didn't boast many opportunities for diversion. The land was gorgeous from up in the air, though. Here, everything existed in shades of brown and gray, with the odd spot of green where piñon pines and junipers had established themselves in the rocky soil. A line of hills rose in the west, a string of striated rocks and stumpy trees. When he took off early in the morning, the sun hit the hills first, and he could see the line between shadow and light thrown into stark relief against them. Then his plane would break that barrier, too, and he'd be washed in the brightness, squinting against the glare. Looking out his cockpit, he could trace the squiggly lines of watercourses that only carried moisture during a hard rain.

He loved watching the shadow of his plane race him back to base, the dark silhouette sliding over the ground, uncatchable.

After primary training they'd been shunted in one of two directions—twin-engine bombers or single-engine fighters. To Frankie's relief, he made it into the fighter group, along with Roy, George, and Ed. Now they were in advanced training and flying the AT-6. They'd also started gunnery practice. A plane towed a long, canvas sleeve along behind it, and they tried to hit it. Everyone had different colored bullets, so they could tell who had scored a hit. George always had yellow, and the canvas usually sported a bright yellow cloudburst. Frankie's green showed up less frequently but enough that he didn't feel like too bad of a shot.

He still hadn't heard any word from David, and he was starting to accept that he probably wouldn't. He had sent him a letter, enclosed in one to his ma, who in turn passed it on to David's mother to include in her next package to him.

Are you stuck in the trenches yet? Seems like
we're never going to get out of training on my end. I
understand why it takes a while, but I'm itching to see
some action. What did you do for Christmas? We had a
"feast," which wasn't much of one. Overdone turkey
and cranberry sauce. They served us the exact same
thing for Thanksgiving. It does beat powdered eggs and
SPAM, though. Do you remember the year it snowed so
much, and we went sledding on the steepest hill we
could find, and I ran into that tree? I still have a little
scar on my chin. Hope I don't pick up any more to add
to the collection.

He'd gone on like that, rambling, not sure what to say. That had been back in January and now it was April and there had only been silence in reply. He thought about Pete a lot too. Frankie was bunking with some guy named Calvin now, whose last name was also Norris. Calvin was civil to him, but Frankie had heard him muttering about the "fruit salad" in the mess hall and decided he didn't want to risk getting too close.

Ed had told him he had found some fellow queers congregating around the chaplain's office and sitting together at meals—the "fruit salad" Calvin had disparaged. But he never pressed Frankie to come sit with them, although Ed did occasionally. It made Frankie feel guilty to avoid them, and yet he also feared the potential consequences.

When they had driven up to the base the first time, his eyes had landed on an enclosure surrounded by wire with a locked and guarded gate. A few men were inside, slouching against the fence or sitting on the ground. A wooden sign nailed over the gate read "Queer Stockade." He had broken out in a sweat and exchanged an agonized glance with Ed, who, as soon as they got off the bus, had whispered to him to play it cool, that everything would be okay. But each morning when they walked to the mess hall, he listened to many of the guys yell insults at the poor bastards who had gotten locked up there. He didn't want to be penned up like that, treated like a weird freak on display in a zoo.

It got worse when Ed got a letter from Dolly with word that Junior had been picked up by the MPs in a "compromising situation." Reading between the lines, it was clear Junior was being questioned by doctors and officers, and they were probably asking him to name names.

Ed had folded the letter slowly, running his thumb along the creases. Frankie had resumed scrubbing his boots, jaw clenched.

"He'll get a blue discharge. He'll have to go home and explain to everyone. Everyone will *know*." Frankie had sucked in a breath. If that happened to him…. "It's not fair."

Ed had nodded. "No, it's not." And then he had fallen silent because it wasn't as though they could do anything about it except pray they didn't get discovered by the wrong person and Junior managed to deflect the questioning.

Apparently he had because they didn't hear anything else about it. But Frankie hadn't let his guard down. It was hard, after the camaraderie on the last base and that wonderful night with Sergio, to be reminded of the harsh reality of the situation. In some ways, that was the worst part—you never knew what you might encounter. Perhaps nobody would care or perhaps you'd get arrested and sent to jail. Frankie tried not to become too anxious and got in as much flying time as possible. When he was up in the air, he left all those other worries behind him. The only thing anyone cared about up here was whether he could pull out of a dive even when the airspeed indicator tipped past the red line.

A FEW weeks later—May 10, 1944, to be exact, a date Frankie would always remember—he stood on the parade ground, back ramrod-straight, eyes forward, and tried not to burst with pride as the CO pinned a pair of silver wings to his uniform. He was officially a Second Lieutenant in the United States Army Air Forces, certified as a fighter pilot. Only transition training remained, when they would finally get to fly the P-51, and then they would be shipped overseas for the real thing.

When the ceremony was over, he had Ed snap a photo of him in his uniform. He'd send one to his family, of course, and also one to Pete. He'd heard from Pete just a few weeks ago. He'd been close to graduating, too, and might already be part of a bomber crew. Pete had told him to have a celebratory drink for him once he'd made pilot, and Frankie intended to make good on that tonight. Although Marana only possessed a few bars, they would do in a pinch.

At five o'clock Frankie made one more check in the mirror to make sure his wings were straight and then headed outside to George's Studebaker, still trundling along gamely despite the hundreds of miles of desert they'd traversed.

"Where's Ed?" Frankie asked, noticing that only Roy and George were there.

"He wasn't feeling so good," George replied. "I told him not to eat too much of those dodgy pork and beans they served us yesterday."

Frankie decided he would smuggle back a bottle of beer for him. There was no way he was going to let Ed miss out on celebrating their ascension to pilot status. In the meantime, though, he had an entire evening of Roy and George's teasing and horseplay to endure by himself. Not that he didn't like Roy and George, for the most part, but he could never completely relax in their company, not like he had been able to with Ed, Junior, and Dolly. But he was used to that—ever since he had realized when he was fourteen that girls didn't do anything for him, he'd had to be careful not to give himself away to the wrong person.

They rolled all the windows down as they drove, trying to pick up a breeze. It already seemed hot, even though it was technically spring. Back home, they could still get snow this time of year. The bar perched on the edge of the city limits. Judging by the number of cars in the lot, it was already crawling with servicemen. They'd just parked when an Oldsmobile pulled up beside them. Two girls climbed out, dressed in blue uniforms, blond and brown hair done in curls under their hats.

47

Roy whistled. "Look here, fellas! We got ourselves a couple of WASPs!"

The girl on the right, who was a little shorter than her companion, raised her eyebrows. "And what are you? Washouts from the base, here to drown your sorrows?"

"You're looking at a trio of top-notch pilots," Roy bragged. "We're leaving tomorrow to get certified in the P-51."

The girl gave them a distinctly unimpressed look. "Well, watch the rudder on your first flight. It's easy to turn too hard, given how responsive the Mustang is compared to those trainers you've gotten used to."

"Sorry?" Roy blinked. "What do you know about flying P-51s, doll?"

"Who do you think ferried them up to the base for you?" she demanded. "And my name is *Lieutenant* Harrison. Come on, Bonnie," she said to the other girl, and they walked into the bar.

"She sure told you what for!" George exclaimed, slapping Roy on the shoulder.

Roy shrugged him off. "Yeah, well, see if I ask her to dance."

"Somehow I don't think she'll mind if you don't," Frankie commented.

"Ah, fuck off," Roy muttered. "Let's get out of the heat and get something to drink."

He led the way inside, Frankie and George following. It wasn't exactly cool in the bar, but the ceiling fans whirred madly and the blinds had been drawn, keeping out the last rays of the setting sun. Roy and George went over to one of the pool tables, but Frankie sat at the bar, sipping his Zombie and just taking a moment to think about the coming days. He'd memorized the controls of the P-51, and now he pictured them in his mind. He imagined the airspeed indicator inching upward, the altimeter climbing.

"Sure you can handle one of those?" It was the WASP from outside, sitting down on the stool next to him and nodding at his drink. "You look kind of skinny." Her friend sat on her other side, giving Frankie a little smile.

Roy had introduced him to the Zombie on a memorable night in March. After spending the day shooting up old Army jeeps and other odd pieces of rusting metal as target practice, Roy had claimed he was "ready for the big stuff." The Zombie did pack a punch— three kinds of rum, apricot brandy, and a variety of fruit juices. Frankie had gotten completely smashed that night and spent all the next morning throwing up.

"I'm just sticking with one," he assured the WASP.

"Do you have better manners than your friend?" she asked.

"Yes, ma'am," he replied, giving her a grin.

Her mouth twitched. "Well, that's a better start at any rate. My name's Iris, and this is—"

"Bonnie. Yeah, I heard." He gave Bonnie a little wave.

"We're based down in Houston," Iris continued. "We're scheduled to fly some P-47s back to base, but we're stuck here for the week until the Jugs are ready. Thought we'd check out the local watering holes."

Bonnie wrinkled her nose. "They leave much to be desired."

Frankie laughed. "Can't argue with that. So you've really flown a Mustang, then? How does the stick respond? I've always found the AT-6 a little sluggish, a little slow to turn. I'm hoping—"

Bonnie chuckled and Iris smiled. "Straight for the shop talk, then?" She exchanged looks with Bonnie. "He's not even going to compliment us on our legs or hair."

"Jeez, I'm sorry," Frankie stammered, blushing. "Your legs... I mean, they're, um...."

"Relax." Iris patted his knee. "We really don't mind. That's usually all we get from fly boys like yourself."

"It's nice that you want to talk to us about the planes instead," Bonnie added. "Although I *did* put on a new shade of lipstick today."

"And you look real pretty in it," Iris told her. "I knew that color would look nice with your hair. Doesn't it...?" She paused. "Actually, I don't think you've told us your name yet."

"Sorry, sorry! I'm Frankie."

"And where are you from, Frankie?" Bonnie asked.

"Little town in Idaho. You?"

"I'm from New Hampshire, and Iris is from Minnesota."

"And boy do we hate Texas!" Iris chimed in. "Blazing hot, and cockroaches as big as your hand all over the barracks."

"Yeah, but you're flying planes," Frankie said. "I'd put up with most anything to do that."

"We both love it," Bonnie agreed.

"And you'll do fine in the P-51," Iris told him. "They're lighter than a Jug. Faster too."

"I like things that go fast. But my friend, Pete, he washed out of the program." Frankie chipped at a crack in the bar with his nail. Pete's absence still hurt after all these months. He hadn't found another close friend and missed having someone to talk to about more serious things. Roy and George were good for a laugh, and Ed was swell, but even though he could be more open with Ed, it still didn't match the friendship he had enjoyed with Pete. Maybe Pete would never have loved him the way Frankie had wanted, but they had still been close. "He kept getting disoriented up in the air."

"I don't think that will happen with you," Bonnie said. "You ever had any problems before?"

Frankie shook his head.

"There you go, then. No reason why the Mustang should be any different."

"Frankie!" It was Roy, slinging an arm around Frankie's shoulder. "Are you hogging the attention of these two lovely ladies?"

"Yeah, let another fellow get a word in edgewise," George said.

"You were busy with your game," Frankie pointed out.

"And who said we wanted to talk to you two?" Iris added. "Are you sure your ego can stand another hit?"

Roy mimed being shot in the chest. "Ouch! Easy there *Lieutenant* Harrison."

"He remembered," Iris said to Bonnie. "I'm shocked. Although I guess his head is big enough to remember the entire encyclopedia."

"Damn, you're just taking them tonight," George said, laughing at Roy.

Roy waved it away. "Why don't we buy these two ladies a drink, Frankie? Maybe they'll be feeling a little friendlier toward us with some gin to ease the way."

Iris and Bonnie both slid off their stools. "Thanks for the offer," Iris said. "But I can't take you up on it. We aren't here looking for romance, just a place to relax for a bit."

"Now, ladies, I don't think that's acceptable," George protested. "We can't have word getting out that we left two gals hanging."

"Aw, just let them go if they want," Frankie interjected. "I want to beat you at pool, anyway."

Roy and George argued a little more, but at last gave it up and dragged Frankie over to the pool table, agreeing that the loser would buy the next round. Iris and Bonnie retired to a booth in the corner and sat by each other, talking softly.

Frankie had his usual game of missed shots and jawed balls. Unlike Ping-Pong, he was abysmal at pool.

By the time he looked up from watching Roy's last ball swirl into the pocket, Iris and Bonnie had disappeared. He bought Roy and George their drinks, enduring their teasing, and then ducked out the door, claiming he needed some air.

The sun had set while they were inside. A yellow glow persisted in the west, the dark mound of a hill outlined against the sky. Frankie lit a cigarette and leaned against the wall. Reaching up, he fingered the wings pinned on his uniform. He still couldn't quite believe he was really done with training, an honest-to-goodness pilot. And the months of training hadn't made him miss the war, either. No, it was still going strong, no end in sight. He wasn't happy about that, but on the other hand, he wanted to see some action. The worst would be going home and admitting you hadn't done anything besides buzz cows and jump fences.

A sound drew Frankie's attention to the parking lot. He could just make out their car and beyond it, Iris and Bonnie's. The two pilots stood there, Bonnie's taller frame leaning over Iris. He was pretty sure they were kissing.

Frankie watched them for a long moment. As he had many times, he flashed back to the feeling of Sergio's mouth against his, and warm, muscled arms curving around his shoulders.

Bonnie laughed softly, and Frankie jerked his eyes away. He stubbed out his cigarette and went back inside. God forbid that Roy or George come out looking for him and see what was going on.

CHAPTER SEVEN

THE FOUR of them packed up the next morning. One long, bumpy ride in George's Studebaker later, and they were at Merced Army Airfield, back in California for transition training. When Frankie climbed out of the car, he just stood there a moment, bag slung over his shoulder, staring at the line of P-51s he could see on the tarmac. He was also glad not to see a separate pen for queers over by the base's prison. Maybe things would be a little more relaxed here.

The rest of the day was spent in the inevitable paperwork and Personnel nonsense. When Frankie went to bed, a similar feeling to the one he remembered from the night before Christmas as a kid possessed him. A grin spread over his face in the dark, as he thought of just how fast he was going to go in that Mustang tomorrow. It took him a long time to fall asleep, and he was up early the next morning.

"Got enough eggs there?" George asked, sitting next to Frankie at breakfast.

Frankie dug in to the mound piled on his plate and shrugged. "You know I like a big meal before flying."

After he'd finished, he wandered out to the hangar, helmet swinging from his fingers. It promised to be warm, and he was already sweating in his bulky flight suit.

The P-51s they were to fly that morning sat gleaming on the runway. They looked massive compared to the AT-6. He sat down on a stack of boxes and ran through the take-off sequence in his head one more time, picturing the controls.

"Hey, move it along, buddy."

Frankie opened his eyes to find a man in a mechanic's uniform standing next to him, cradling a box in his arms.

"I have to set this down right where you're sitting," the man continued.

"Sorry." Frankie got up and stood aside. The man deposited his box and then looked at Frankie, brown eyes flicking over him.

"Haven't you got somewhere to be?" he asked.

Frankie tilted his chin up. "Why? This hangar your own personal property?"

"No." The brown eyes settled into a glare. "But you're interfering with my work."

"Oh, sure. Moving boxes. Looks *real* difficult," Frankie drawled.

The guy shook his head. "Figures. You pilots think you're so damn superior to everybody else. Well, let me tell you something, hotshot, you'd be nose down in a ditch if it wasn't for the aircrews."

"I never said I was superior!" Frankie replied, stung. "The only one acting superior here is you—strutting about like you own the place."

"You sure your head is gonna fit in that helmet?" The guy started walking away. "Maybe you should get your ass in gear and go do something useful. This ain't no vacation you signed up for!"

"Yeah, I know that!" Frankie shouted after him. "Asshole," he muttered, jogging in the opposite direction toward the ready room where the squadron was assembling.

The CO explained that first they would be flying individually before trying anything as a group. They were supposed to fly a big circle around the base. The CO glared down at the assembled pilots as he stressed that they were not to try any tricks, rolls, or dives on their first flight. He told them a suitably grim story about a pilot who had done so and ended up crashing his plane, nothing left but a burning tangle of metal. Still, Frankie could tell it didn't have quite the desired effect on the audience, which was too wired to be put off by such tales.

Frankie's heart thudded as he approached the P-51. It loomed over him, thirteen feet high. Trying to work some spit into his mouth to ease his dry throat, he clambered up onto the wing and swung into the cockpit. This was it. This was *it*. Speeds of 437 mph? He could already feel the engine humming under him.

He was trying to get settled in the seat and get his oxygen tube in the right place when a hand clapped onto his shoulder.

"Need some help there?"

The voice seemed familiar, and a second later, Frankie found himself looking up into the face of the mechanic he had encountered earlier.

"I'm Jim Morrow," the guy said after a moment, mouth thinning into a hard line. "And I'm the chief of your aircrew."

"Oh." *Fuck* he added in his head but didn't say aloud because his ma had trained him better than that. "I'm Frankie Norris."

Jim shoved roughly at his shoulders, yanking the straps down.

"I'm fine," Frankie muttered, trying to bat him away. "Wouldn't want to distract you from your *real* work."

Jim rolled his eyes. "Figures I'd get you. Well, just don't crash your first time out, okay? I'd hate to lose this beauty I've worked so hard on."

He jumped off the wing before Frankie could come up with a retort.

Frankie sat there stewing for a moment, but now was not the time to get tied in knots over having a jerk for an aircrew chief. Taking a deep breath, he focused on the instrument panel, everything laid out exactly like the boards he had spent so long memorizing. When he started the plane, all 1,650 horsepower of the Packard Merlin engine roared to life, his heart jumping at the noise and the sheer power thrumming around him. Just think of doing a Cuban eight in this baby....

But he'd behave this time and stick to the basics. Checking that the magneto switches were on, he released the brakes and advanced the throttle, rumbling out onto the runway. When the tower gave him the go-ahead, he started picking up speed, and then he was airborne. Swinging his eyes over the instruments, he saw they all checked out. Jim must be a pretty good mechanic. Frankie was both very glad of that fact and a little disappointed he wouldn't have anything to rag Jim over.

The Mustang responded beautifully to all his commands. He tried the trick that Hollen had shown him once, applying the rudder while keeping the wings level so the plane slipped sideways. It wasn't *really* a trick, not like a snap roll or a hammerhead stall. And he couldn't resist pushing the throttle, building up speed, edging toward that red line. The g-forces pressed him back in his seat, and he knew he was grinning like a fool. This—it was better than he had dreamed.

He should have remembered what Hollen told him about landings always being the most difficult part, though. After, he wasn't quite sure what went wrong. All he knew was that one minute he was heading in for a textbook landing, and the next he had missed his mark and was going to have to go round again. If that wasn't bad enough, he missed the *second* time, too, unable to coordinate everything and find that perfect moment to set the wheels down. He finally stuck the landing the third time, but he knew his face was burning with embarrassment. He unbuckled his straps, wrenched his helmet off, and popped the top. When he stood up, he saw Jim standing under the plane, grinning up at him.

"Don't say one damn word," Frankie warned, because even his ma's lessons in manners couldn't hold for situations like this.

"Wasn't going to," Jim replied, looking delighted. "Just wondering if you actually *had* any flying lessons or if you skipped that part of pilot training."

"So I missed the landing!" Frankie's boots hit the ground with a thud. "Other than that it was the perfect flight."

"Well, if you could just stay up in the air all the time, I might agree with you. But you see, there's this pesky thing called fuel that planes need."

"Jeez, thanks for the information." Frankie pushed past him and headed toward Captain Haley, who was frowning in his direction. Haley had survived his 250 mission hours in Italy and had now been given the job of teaching new pilots in the hope they would survive theirs too.

Frankie couldn't tell if Haley was pleased or irritated by the assignment.

"Maybe you should go back to that farm in Kansas," Jim called after him.

"I'm not from a farm, and I'm not from Kansas!" Frankie yelled back.

Haley chewed him out, and Frankie mumbled "yes, sir," and "no, sir," at appropriate intervals.

"Hard luck," Roy sympathized with him afterward, when they were collapsed back in their barracks, going over the flight. "I almost clipped a truck on the takeoff. Damn, those planes are big ass beauties."

"They're perfect." Frankie's discontent melted into a grin, thinking back over how it had felt to be up in the air in a state-of-the-art fighter plane.

Roy laughed. "I caught a glimpse of you. Thought you were going to head right out over the Pacific."

"Yeah, I didn't want to come back. I just wanted to keep going faster and farther," Frankie admitted.

"Next week gunnery practice starts," George commented. "That's what *I'm* looking forward to."

"You're a bloodthirsty son of a bitch," Roy told him.

George shrugged. "You gotta be. It's a war, right?"

"Think any of us will be aces?" Frankie asked, thinking it over. He didn't want to kill people, exactly, but George was right—it was a war, and you had to do what needed to be done.

"We can think about that once we survive a couple of missions," Ed put in, looking up from his book. "The first thing is not to get killed. Then you can worry about putting bullets in other people."

"Christ, Ed," Roy muttered. "We all know the odds, right? So why talk about it?"

"There's a difference between being smart and getting scared," Frankie said. "Captain Haley's always talking about being alert and aware of your surroundings and judging the situation. And he had to be doing something right."

Roy shrugged. "Sometimes I just don't want to think about it, I guess. Now come on, who's in for a game of poker?"

THE NEXT morning, when Frankie entered the canteen, he spotted Jim right away. Jim was leaning his chair against the wall, legs swinging, laughing with his buddies. Then he noticed Frankie.

"Well, if it isn't the rube from Kansas!" Jim exclaimed. "Got the hayseeds out of your ears yet?"

Frankie ignored him and went and collected his tray of eggs and sticky oatmeal. He avoided looking Jim's way while he ate. Of course, this was only delaying the inevitable.

Sure enough, when he got to his plane, Jim climbed up onto the wing to help him get situated in the cockpit again.

"I can handle it," Frankie snapped.

Jim gave him a smug grin. "The evidence suggests otherwise." He rapped his knuckles on Frankie's helmet and jumped down.

Christ, he was annoying.

Frankie pushed Jim from his mind and paid attention to his preflight checklist. Then he eased the throttle forward, received the all clear, and lifted off. He wished he could waggle his wings a bit, maybe try a dive. But that kind of stuff would get him kicked out, so he restrained the impulse and instead concentrated on having the perfect flight—including the landing. This time he went farther, although the ocean was still a ways off, too far to go hunt for submarines.

When he got back to base, the landing went off without a hitch. He taxied to a halt and gave Jim, who was standing on the edge of the runway, a cheeky wave.

Jim was already moving toward the plane to check it over by the time Frankie got unstrapped and back on the ground.

"I was kind of hoping you'd get lost," Jim said, twirling a screwdriver in his hands.

But Frankie had just had a perfect flight, and he turned a grin back at him. "Make sure you know which end goes where," he said, nodding at the screwdriver, and then walked off, whistling. Haley gave him an approving grunt when Frankie checked in and said that tomorrow he would begin doing formation flying with the rest of the squadron.

Feeling jubilant, he dashed off a quick letter to his family—*just finished my second flight in the P-51. You wouldn't believe how fast it goes. I'm glad to be back in California weather. Arizona was too warm for me, although I guess Merced gets pretty hot in the summer. Tell Helen I hope they were able to find a better place to live and aren't crammed into that apartment anymore.* His oldest sister, Helen, and her husband had moved to Richmond, up by San Francisco, a few months into the war. Her husband had gotten a job as a welder at the Kaiser Shipyards, but with so many new workers flooding the area, housing had been pretty scarce. Helen and her three little kids were stuck in a small apartment. The government was building housing, though, and Helen thought they might be able to get a place.

He couldn't help but grin again, thinking of his two nieces and one nephew—Judy, Beatrice, and Oliver. Judy, the oldest, was only five, but he hadn't seen any of them since Christmas two years ago, and he bet he'd hardly recognize them now, they must be getting so big. Frankie liked kids, and that Christmas he had spent most of it carting Judy around on his shoulders and helping her build snowmen. *Tell Judy I want her to pick up some seashells for me, and I promise to bring her a souvenir from wherever I get posted. I should know where I'll be headed soon. I'm not sure I'll be able to tell you exactly, but at least I'll know if it's going to be Europe or the Pacific.*

Sealing the envelope, he tucked the letter into his jacket and wandered off to see if he could find a snack, stomach rumbling and too hungry to wait another hour until dinner.

CHAPTER EIGHT

THE NEXT day he came out onto the airfield early. Jim and the rest of his crew were at the plane, checking it over and making adjustments.

"Hey," Frankie said, and Jim looked at him, squinting against the sun.

"What do you want?" he demanded. "Your plane will be ready at 1330, when you're scheduled to fly. I don't need you coming out to check up on me."

Frankie bit back a smart-ass reply. "That's not why I'm here. I just want to watch what you're doing, maybe ask some questions. I want to get to know my plane."

Jim gave him a long stare. "All right," he finally said. "Cooper, show Dorothy here everything he didn't know he needed to know about radiators and engines."

"I am *not* from Kansas," Frankie growled. Wishing *The Wizard of Oz* hadn't been so popular that even someone like Jim had seen it, he followed Cooper—a short gray-haired man in oil-stained coveralls—around to the other side of the plane.

"You'll have heard all kinds of shit in those classes," Cooper began, "but there's a lot of tricks they don't tell you about. Now see this hose here...."

Frankie bent close, listening, but he glanced back once and caught Jim watching them. Jim mouthed "Dorothy" at him again and then ducked out of sight.

"So where are you really from, then?" Jim asked later, when he was helping Frankie get strapped into the cockpit.

"Idaho," Frankie replied. "A little town near Pocatello. My father owns a ranch."

"It's a pretty story, but you can't erase Kansas from your blood." Jim rapped his knuckles on Frankie's helmet again.

"Dammit, will you stop that?" Frankie demanded, but Jim just jumped off, chuckling.

"I'm telling the truth, you know," Frankie said when he returned from the flight. He watched as Jim studied the wing flaps, frowning and testing one of the screws. "I can show you the letters from my mother, postmarked in Idaho."

"Hey, I get why you're embarrassed. I wouldn't want to admit I came from Kansas, either. But you can't hide it, Frankie, so you might as well tell the truth. Be... frank about it."

"Ha-ha. Like I haven't heard that one a hundred times. What about you?"

"What about me?"

"Where are you from? Or did you just spring from the tarmac one day for the sole purpose of being a pain in my ass?"

Jim snorted and wiped his hands on a rag. He wore a short-sleeved shirt, and his arms and face had gotten tanned by the sun. His brown hair stuck to his neck in sweaty clumps. "I'm from Los Angeles. And I take it as a compliment—being a pain in your ass. I live to pop the inflated egos of pilots."

"Your own could use a little deflating."

Jim tapped him on the shoulder with his wrench. "A word to the wise—you should butter up your crew chief. After all, I'm the one making sure the plane doesn't fall apart around you."

Frankie raised his eyebrows. "You think I don't see how much you love this plane? The plane is what you care about. You'll make sure she gets back in one piece. I don't think you give a shit about me."

"Well, it would be one less annoyance in my day, not having to put up with you," Jim drawled.

Frankie glared and went off to the pilot's lounge to try and find something cool to drink. He guessed Jim was somewhere in his early twenties. The few years he had on Frankie didn't give him the license to act so damn superior.

"Hey, Frankie!" Roy waved him over. He and Ed were sitting at a table, smoking and drinking some coffee, a newspaper spread out between them. "Guess what?" Roy continued when Frankie sat down next to him. "Some of the guys are putting on a girlie show tomorrow night."

"You mean with... dresses and stuff?"

Roy nodded. "Should be pretty swell." He laughed. "Can't you just see old Larry in a wig?"

"I just hope their dresses aren't too short," Ed said. "Having to watch Larry's skinny legs kicking up and down, that's enough to give you nightmares right there."

"The CO is actually okay with this?" Frankie asked, a little stunned that the Army was sanctioning drag shows. Although come to think of it, there was that entire production—*This Is the Army*—that had toured the U.S. and overseas, and there were plenty of men playing women in it and wearing dresses and wigs. He'd seen a write-up in the newspaper about it last year. But the emphasis had all been on the humor and the fact that the actors, who were all active-duty soldiers, were just as ready to fight as they were to dance. The writer might as well have written in big block print: "No Fairies Here."

"Yep, the CO said it was fine," Roy continued. "I mean, maybe we'll be lucky and the USO will bring out Tommy Tucker and his orchestra to entertain us, but until such a time, we gotta make do with what we got."

Frankie fell silent, wondering how he should react to this and thankful no one had asked him to participate. Would showing too much interest be taken as a sign that he was queer? But no, Roy was talking about it and making jokes. As long as he treated it the same way, he should be in the clear.

Accordingly, the next night he joined the crowd gathering in the mess hall, which had been converted into an auditorium—standing room only—with a plywood stage at one end. At last, the lights went down and the band struck up a tune. Frankie thought he recognized it, but it wasn't until a second lieutenant stepped up to the mike on stage and began to sing that he recollected the lyrics.

He'd first heard it back in Idaho last summer, when he and his ma had gone to see a movie one night. "I need a date for the evening, Frankie," she had said. "So put on a nice shirt and wash your face." The movie was called *The Fleet's In* and was about sailors wooing a girl in some port. He had heard this song on the radio a couple of times since then.

The soldier preparing to sing was Webster Collins, one of the few on base who could hold a tune, according to rumor. He started to sing in a wavering voice, looking slightly nervous. But he warmed up to the tune about the girl called "Tangerine," who made all the men sigh and the women green with envy, and soon he was winking at the audience and grinning.

The crowd started laughing, catching on to what was coming. The curtain on the side of the stage, held up on a jury-rigged system of metal poles, twitched and then was flung aside. If the beans hadn't been spilled by a few guys earlier that day, Frankie wouldn't have been able to guess who came sashaying onto the stage.

"Victor is going to be playing the lead," they had said, laughing. Frankie had tried to picture it—Victor, who could throw a baseball farther than any guy on base, putting on a dress and acting like a girl. It had sounded ludicrous. But now, seeing him up there on the stage....

Victor wore a bright red dress—God only knew where they had gotten it—that had lots of ruffles in the skirt. It hung low on his chest, and his arms bulged out of it. He carried a fan that he waved seductively, and he had a wig on his head, covering up his short hair. He sported lipstick, too, and maybe even eye shadow; Frankie couldn't be sure. It was the way he walked, though, swinging his hips in time to the music, and coyly tilting his head. It looked feminine, despite the muscles and dark hair on his arms.

Victor sidled up to Webster, draping his arm over his shoulders and kissing his ear to much hooting and hollering. Webster's face was red, but he kept singing, finishing up the song.

Then the band switched to "Comin' In on a Wing and a Prayer," and the curtains gave way to an entire chorus line, all dolled up and kicking their legs.

They belted out the song, making up in enthusiasm what they lacked in talent. Victor danced in the front, kicking up his legs just as high and flashing his thigh at the audience, half of whom had joined in on the singing.

Frankie had laughed along with everyone else amid the wolf whistles that pierced the air, and now he tried to sing, but his voice didn't do more than croak in the back of his throat. He couldn't look away from Victor. Because Victor was a pansy. Frankie was sure of it. The way he moved his hips. The lilt in his voice. He had to be.

Nobody seemed to give a shit, either, and he suspected that once the show was over, and the makeup came off, everyone would go back to treating Victor like he was one of the guys, like they always had.

Frankie's stomach twisted, and he scrubbed his hands along his pants. Part of him kind of liked the idea of Victor in a dress, and he had a sudden vivid image of Victor with his skirt shoved up around his waist, ass bare. Or maybe just Victor without the dress, in a white undershirt instead, short hair tousled. And maybe it would be Victor behind him, instead, bending him over. Or maybe Pete—

Christ, he had to stop this. His pants were getting tight at the crotch, and he'd have a full-blown erection if he didn't watch it. And wouldn't that be just great—to get hard during a girlie show. Oh God, if Roy or George noticed....

Swallowing back his panic, Frankie started shoving his way out of the audience, heading toward the door. Guys stepped aside, irritated, a few asking him why he was leaving now, just when it was getting good.

Frankie ignored them and at last stumbled outside. He walked a few feet away and then bent over, hands on his knees, trying to slow his breaths.

"Too much for a country boy to handle, huh?"

It was Jim. Just what he didn't need right now. "Shut up and leave me alone."

"What's eating you?" Jim lit a cigarette, the match a bright flare in the darkness.

"It was just too hot and... crowded," Frankie muttered. He straightened up and frowned. "Why are you here?"

Jim shrugged. "I've seen better."

"Better... drag shows?"

"Yeah. There was this one bar in LA. All the fairies and queens went there. They held pansy balls sometimes, if things had cooled down enough with the cops."

"And you went to them?"

Jim laughed. "Lots of people went."

"Oh."

"And those queens, they sure looked spiffy." Jim waved at the mess hall. "This lot are rank amateurs next to them. 'Sides, like you said, it was blamed hot in there."

Frankie wanted to ask Jim more about this bar, ask him if he had actually known any of the drag queens, and ask him what he thought of Victor. But if he started asking questions, Jim might start asking questions back, and that couldn't end well.

"I know it must be a shock for someone who's only seen cornfields and cows his whole life. Bet your mama never even let you go out alone with a girl."

"I had a girlfriend!" Frankie shot back. He'd taken Ruth Baxter to a few movies and school dances. They had kissed twice, and he had put his hand on her breast once and then snatched it back. She had blushed and stared out the car window instead of at him. Neither of them had talked about it, and she broke up with him after graduation.

He hadn't felt too cut up about it. After all, every time he went to pick her up at her house, quietly praying that the old Ford Runabout didn't die on him, he spent most of the time hoping Ruth's older brother, Michael, would be there. Michael had been in his late twenties, and he usually didn't pay much attention to Frankie, but sometimes he'd say hello or shoot a smile their way. Frankie's heart always sped up under the influence of Michael's broad shoulders and quiet hazel eyes.

"Bet you've never been with a girl, though," Jim continued mercilessly. "I bet you're still a virgin."

"Well, you're wrong," Frankie snapped back, but Jim just laughed, unconvinced.

Frankie glared. "Glad I could furnish you with some entertainment. Christ, you're such a jerk." He hunched his shoulders and spun around, then set off toward the hangars. He'd walk around a bit and then go back inside. He could say he had needed to take a leak if anyone asked.

Jim's voice floated after him. "Sweet dreams, Dorothy!"

CHAPTER NINE

ROY DIVED for the ball but missed. It pinged off the table and bounced along the floor. Frankie whooped and pumped his fist. "Is that what you call your A-game, Roy?"

"Now you owe me a dollar," George added from where he was sitting against the wall, watching their Ping-Pong game.

"You know I don't have any money 'til we get paid," Roy told him and then turned back to Frankie. "And you, couldn't you have gone easy on a fella, for once?"

The door to the rec room opened, and Frankie watched as Jim and some other mechanics entered, heading for the dart board. "Hey, I have to maintain my title as Ping-Pong champion," he said, turning his attention back to Roy. "Honor of the squadron and all that."

"Give me a rematch at least. Let me win some of my money back from George."

George guffawed. "It's just going to put you deeper in the hole."

Frankie glanced over to the other side of the room and thought Jim was watching him, but the next second, Jim shouldered his way into position, a dart poised in his fingers. Frankie jerked back around to the Ping-Pong table. "Sure, I'll play you again. But you're not gonna beat me."

"Pride cometh before a fall," Roy shot back and served quickly.

Frankie lunged for the ball, settling into the rhythm. He beat Roy even faster this time.

"Mercy!" Roy cried, pretending to be hit in the chest. He sprawled over the table. "Take pity on me, O cruel one."

"You're the one asking for it," Frankie replied, smiling and hauling him to his feet. "Come on, George, let's go cheer him up."

"Hold on a minute," a voice said, and he turned to find Jim standing there, dart game abandoned. "Care to play a real opponent?"

"Hey!" Roy began, outraged, but Frankie cut him off.

"You think you're that good, huh?"

"I know I'm that good," Jim returned.

George whistled. "Show him the error of his ways, Frankie."

"Yeah, all right." Frankie handed Jim the paddle Roy had been using. "Just don't say I never warned you."

Jim grinned. "Famous last words, Dorothy."

"For the last time," Frankie said, slamming the ball down the table, "I am not from Kansas!"

Then they couldn't talk, too absorbed in following the quick movements of the ball. It darted back and forth. Frankie almost missed one, misjudging the swing, but managed to catch it in time. Jim was good—better than Roy, certainly. At last Frankie sent a ball whizzing so fast that Jim just couldn't get there soon enough.

Roy and George cheered and slapped him on the back. Frankie grinned and panted, chest heaving.

Jim stared stony-faced at Frankie for a moment, but then a smile slowly spread across his face. "Good game."

"Thanks," Frankie said, startled but pleased. "You too."

Jim nodded. "See you around, then," he said and jogged back over to rejoin the dart game.

"Not a very talkative guy, is he?" Roy observed.

"He can be when he wants to," Frankie replied, remembering some of Jim's choicer insults. He watched as Jim threw and the dart thumped into the cork.

"Come on, Frankie, let's hit the showers," George said, and Frankie turned away to follow them, musing on this new side of Jim, a Jim who smiled and didn't insult Frankie with every breath he took.

THE NEXT time he stumbled on Jim, he was taking a shortcut behind a utility shed to get to his meteorology class. He literally almost tripped over him because Jim was propped up against an old barrel, taking a nap. Jim blinked awake at the sound of Frankie's cursing.

"Hey," he said, stretching and shading his eyes against the sun.

"You know if you get caught, it'll be demerits," Frankie told him.

"I never get caught." Jim fished into his pocket and pulled out a packet of Mallo Cups. He ripped it open and popped one of the coconut-filled chocolates into his mouth. "Want one? They got a little melted, but they're still good."

"Um, no thanks, I have to get to class."

Jim hummed and shut his eyes again.

After that, Frankie noticed Jim often took little catnaps whenever the opportunity presented itself. Two days later, when Jim met him after he came in from a flight, he saw Jim hiding a yawn. "Did I wake you up?" he teased.

"I fell asleep because you were taking so long out there," Jim retorted. "You know these things go faster than forty miles per hour, right?"

"Yeah, I got that figured out." Frankie grinned. "It's my favorite part. You know in Kansas, we all drive buggies. Can't go faster than a brisk trot at best."

Jim laughed. "See? Knew you would admit to your native state someday."

JOKING ASIDE, Frankie did like going fast, and now they were getting to do mock dogfights in addition to air-to-air gunnery and dive bombing.

"Stay in formation, Red Two," the flight instructor's voice said, crackling over the radio, and Frankie pulled back, slipping in behind Roy, even though he itched to zoom ahead. Blue Flight was waiting for them somewhere up ahead, and he kept craning his neck, looking up into the sun.

Finally Ed's voice snapped, "Bogies, two o'clock high."

"Red flight, engage," their instructor said.

Frankie snap rolled to the left and then pulled up sharply. A plane hurtled past his right side, and he turned, trying to get on its tail. The pilot dropped down and flipped over, intending to circle around and come up behind Frankie. But Frankie followed him, adrenaline surging as he suddenly found himself looking up at the ground. Then he righted himself, but his opponent had disappeared.

Cursing, he targeted a plane following closely on Ed's tail. "I'm on my way, Red Four," he said, gunning the throttle. The other pilot was so intent that he didn't even notice Frankie for a good minute. Frankie pretended to fire the guns, concentrating on keeping the target centered.

"Got a kill," he said to Jim back on the field, hopping a little as the excitement of the fight lingered.

"And look at the stress you put on the damn aileron," Jim muttered. "Are you actually trying to break my plane?"

"Your plane?" Frankie laughed. "She is definitely *my* plane."

"No, you just get to borrow her occasionally. I'm the one who provides the care and feeding, and slaves over her after you try to tear her to pieces."

"Hey, if your little delusions make you happy," Frankie said and walked off, laughing at Jim's glare.

IF HE didn't know better, Frankie would have thought Jim was following him around. He seemed to run into his crew chief everywhere. Even his barracks weren't immune, as one afternoon Jim appeared out of the blue, poking his head around the door and asking, "Want to shoot some hoops?"

Frankie groaned. "Does it look like I want to play basketball?" he demanded, gesturing at the heavy wool dress uniform he had worn while marching off some demerits, thanks to a scrap he had gotten into with some guys from another squadron the day before. With the end of their training drawing near, tempers were running high as everyone waited on tenterhooks to find out where they would be posted. He couldn't even remember how the fight had started, only that it sure had been nice to release some tension and throw a few punches. Now, after marching for two hours, it seemed like a pretty stupid thing to have done. He was sweaty and exhausted but had flight training in an hour that he couldn't miss. "I don't have time anyway."

"Hmmm." Jim wandered over and flipped through the stack of postcards Frankie had scattered around. Frankie snatched them back.

"Hey, those are private."

Jim raised an eyebrow. "Love letters? You got a gal back in Kansas?"

"No. They're from my mother. Mostly."

"Oh, a momma's boy." Jim grinned. "Should have known. Are you even shaving yet, Dorothy?"

"Would you scram?" Frankie snapped. "Go do whatever it is you're supposed to be doing. Like looking after my plane." He had taken off his uniform coat and now stripped off his sweaty undershirt, searching for a dry one.

"A dollar says I can shoot more baskets than you," Jim said, moving a few feet away but lingering.

Frankie snorted. "Fine, I'll play you tomorrow. But your wallet will be lighter when we're done."

JIM MOVED fast on the court, keeping easy control of the ball as it bounced between his feet. But Frankie had the height advantage and always grabbed the rebounds. After thirty minutes Jim sagged against the wall, panting, and called a halt to the game.

"Don't smirk," he said, handing Frankie a dollar.

Frankie held up his hands. "I'm not. I won't even say I told you so."

"First Ping-Pong, now basketball." Jim shook his head, but he seemed to be taking his loss with good grace.

"You played really well. I'm just taller than you."

"By two inches *at the most*." Jim crossed his arms over his chest, giving Frankie a once-over. "'Sides, you're dang skinny. I could probably knock you over with one hand."

"You could try," Frankie retorted, instantly on the defensive, curling his hand into a fist.

"Hey. Easy, Dorothy." Jim grabbed his shoulder and gave him a little shake. "I'm not looking to pick a fight. I enjoyed our game. We'll have to play again sometime."

Frankie shrugged, abashed.

"I know why you're wound so tight," Jim continued. "You're hoping to find out where you'll be posted so you can get the hell out of here. Just like the rest of us."

Frankie nodded. "I'm sick of waiting. I want to get my first mission over with so I can stop thinking about it."

Jim put a hand on his back and propelled him toward the door. "What you need is a stiff drink. Let's go into town. I can borrow my buddy Roger's car."

"I don't know," Frankie began, not sure he wanted to spend an entire evening in Jim's company. Although he had to admit that in the past few days, Jim's insults had come to lack the bite they had originally possessed. Now they were almost... fond, and instead of a spike of irritation whenever he saw Jim, Frankie had almost started to look forward to their interactions. He wasn't sure what to make of it. He had horsed around with and teased David and Pete, of course, but with Jim it was somehow different. Frankie couldn't figure if Jim thought of him as a friend or if he was still just someone who provided a handy source of amusement half the time and had to be tolerated the other half.

"Aw, come on," Jim pleaded, and he looked so genuinely disappointed that Frankie gave in.

It turned out they wouldn't be alone, anyway, because Roger wanted to come, and then two more guys caught wind of the scheme, and so he ended up crammed in the back of Roger's car, while Jim sat up front in the passenger seat and fiddled with the radio.

"So you're Jimmy's pilot, huh?" Roger shouted over the sounds of "They're Either Too Young or Too Old."

"Uh, yes," Frankie replied.

"Well go easy on that plane, would you?" Roger continued. "Jimmy won't shut up about it. Drives me nuts."

Frankie stayed silent, not sure how to reply to this.

"Says you did an Immelmann yesterday that practically took off a wing."

"I did not," Frankie protested loudly as a trumpet blared.

"Can't do that kind of roll, huh?" the guy on his right said. Frankie couldn't remember his name. Webster? Wallace?

"No, I did the roll, but I didn't—"

"I could never hack it with all those twists and turns," Wallace said, interrupting. "I'd puke up my guts all over. You ever done that?"

"No." Frankie tried to shift into a more comfortable position. Jim was staring out the window, one foot propped on the dashboard, apparently uninterested in the conversation. Frankie thought this was a bit rude, seeing as how Jim had talked him into going to town in the first place.

"My stomach, it's real sensitive," Wallace continued. "I eat one wrong thing, and that's it. Like artichokes. Boy, I can't stand artichokes."

"Will you shut up about your stomach, Woodrow?" the guy on Frankie's other side said. "Christ."

"The doctor even warned me about it," Wallace—no, Woodrow said, soldiering on, undaunted. "He said, 'Private, if you don't want to end up in sick bay for a month, you'll stay away from that chili powder.'"

"Maybe that cute gal Melanie will be at the bar again," Roger said, oblivious to Woodrow's sorrows. "I almost got her the last time. A few more kisses, and I would have been home free." He slapped his hand on the steering wheel. "She's stacked too!"

Woodrow leaned closer to Frankie. "And then there was the one time I ate the mango."

Smothering a sigh, Frankie let his head drop back against the seat.

When they finally got there, the bar smelled of heat and stale smoke. Frankie grabbed a beer—no way was he trusting himself to

Jim's tender mercies if he got smashed—and sat at a booth in a corner. Jim found him a few seconds later.

"So, that dollar," he began, "could I, um, borrow some back?"

Frankie stared at him. "You have got to be kidding. You want me to loan you the money I just won from you?"

"That's about the size of it, yeah."

Blowing out an exasperated breath, Frankie pulled out his wallet. "You could have just not played the game with me, you know. It would have been a hell of a lot easier than playing the game, getting beat, and then convincing me to come here so you could get your money back."

"That's not why I asked you," Jim protested. "I forgot I didn't have any more cash. I didn't bring you here just to pay for my drinks, Frankie."

"Could have fooled me," Frankie muttered.

Jim hesitated and then sat down across from him. He ignored the dollar bill Frankie held out. "It's true. And I didn't mean for those idiots to come along, either." He waved his hand at Roger and the others, who were chatting up two girls at the bar.

Frankie studied Jim's expression and then nodded. "We'll call it even if you sit by Woodrow on the way back."

"You don't make it easy to get back in your good graces, do you?"

"I didn't think you cared about being in them."

Jim shrugged. "I need someone to fly that plane after all the work I put into it. And you're not the worst pilot I could have been stuck with."

"Gee, thanks," Frankie said dryly.

"That Roy Kozlowski fellow, for example."

"Hey, lay off Roy," Frankie protested. "And take the damn dollar and go get yourself a beer."

Jim returned to the booth after doing so and handed Frankie the change. "That girl over there is making eyes at you," he said, nodding at a blond in a white sundress. "Now that's definitely a way to relax. She'd make you forget all about where they're going to send you."

Frankie took a careful swallow of his beer. He should agree. He should go over and talk to the girl and dance with her. "Maybe another time."

Jim watched him for a long moment and then shrugged and took a swig of his beer in turn. "So where do you think they'll send us?"

"Maybe Italy. But it might be the Eighth Air Force, too, over in Britain. We just stormed the beaches at Normandy and got a little foothold in France, after all." It had been all over the papers a week ago, the headlines screaming about the D-Day invasion. "I figure they'll be looking for more pilots to go on raids deeper into Germany."

Jim nodded. "You have any brothers fighting?"

"No. I have two older sisters, and my little brother is four years younger than I am. God, I hope the war is over before he turns eighteen."

"My older brother is in the Army. Somewhere in the Pacific, last I heard." Jim took another drink. "He thinks I should be fighting instead of 'sitting on my ass fixing propellers,' as he put it."

"Well, that's just dumb. If we couldn't fix the planes, we couldn't fly them or fight them."

"Oh, so you do appreciate me." Jim gave Frankie a grin.

Frankie huffed. "A bit. Maybe."

Jim laughed.

"So why did you decide to go into aircraft maintenance?" Frankie asked, curious to know more about Jim.

"My uncle owns an auto repair shop," Jim replied, leaning back against the wall and stretching out his right leg along the seat. "He took care of us after my mom and dad died. I started working there when I was, oh, probably eleven. Since I already knew my way around a screwdriver, the Big Wheels decided fixing planes was how I could best serve my country."

Frankie thought of asking what had happened to Jim's parents, but he didn't want to sound morbidly curious. "Will you go back to it, after the war?"

"I guess." Jim took another swallow of beer. "I never did so well at school. Only other thing I can think of doing is playing basketball, but I'm not tall enough that anyone would ever pay me to do it."

"I think I might like to stay with the Air Forces. If it meant I could keep flying."

"You love it that much, huh?"

Frankie nodded, drumming his fingers on the table.

Jim looked at him a moment and then tilted his head against the wall, closing his eyes. "I have to admit that you aren't too shabby at it. Although I think they need pilots so bad they'll take anyone who can get a plane off the ground and stay up for twenty minutes."

"Your confidence is so inspiring."

A smile crept over Jim's mouth, and he raised his beer to Frankie.

Frankie finished off his own beer and then ran his thumb around the rim, pensive. Suddenly a thought occurred to him, and he sat up. "Jeepers, I just realized you'll be coming with me to wherever I get posted."

Jim snorted and cracked open his eyes. "I am your crew chief. That's the whole point of transition training, to get all of us working together as a cohesive squadron. Did you think I was going to foist you off on some other poor bastard? I've already composed a letter of condolence to whatever plane gets assigned to you."

"Oh God." Frankie slumped back. "I'm going to have to deal with your Kansas jokes my entire tour, aren't I?"

Jim grinned. "Hey, you know what they say—war is hell."

ON THE way back to the base, Jim did sit next to Woodrow as promised. Frankie sat in front and let the night breeze wash over him through the open window, drowning out the sounds of the others' chatter. When they returned, he waved good night. Jim looked like he wanted to talk some more, but Roger grabbed his arm, and Frankie seized the opportunity to jog off. Jim sometimes put him on edge. Tonight had been all right, and he guessed he could call Jim his friend now. But there was still something different about the way

Jim looked at him and talked to him. For a second he entertained the wild notion that maybe Jim was attracted to him. He pictured those dark brown eyes sliding shut, Jim tilting his head up for a kiss. But no. Frankie shut that thought down fast, even as a curl of lust tightened his stomach. He'd already been through this once with Pete. No way was Jim queer. He wasn't going to go through the heartache of pining after someone who just wanted to be friends. Shrugging it off, Frankie swerved aside from the path to the barracks and went to the darkened hangar instead.

He leaned against the metal wall, looking out over the landing strip. A light shone in the control tower, and up above, the stars covered the sky, half-obscured by a fat moon hanging low in the west.

Frankie wished he could just hop in a plane and take off, skimming low over the fields, admiring the lights of towns swirling together in bright clusters.

He wondered what anti-aircraft fire would be like. All the flak bursting around him.

Two hundred and fifty hours flying missions.

Well, there was no point thinking about it. If he was meant to survive, he would survive. And in the meantime, he'd fly the hell out of that Mustang.

CHAPTER TEN

THE OCEAN liner had been a luxury passenger ship before the war. Now it held over five thousand GIs crammed together, sometimes eighteen to a stateroom, sleeping in three shifts of six. Thank God the trip to Britain only took about a week, Frankie reflected, leaning on the railing and looking down at the long drop to the heaving waves of the Atlantic below. He already felt stir crazy, not to mention the itching fear that a U-Boat could torpedo them out of the water at any second.

They'd finally received word they were being sent to Britain to join the Eighth Air Force. Two weeks of monotonous train rides across the country ensued, followed by a confused jumble of "hurrying up and waiting" once they got to New York. At last they boarded the ship and set off. Frankie was sharing a room with Ed and some other guys from their squadron who he didn't know too well beyond their last names. Roy and George were somewhere else in the maze of passageways. Frankie thought he had glimpsed George's red hair through a sea of khaki at dinner the other day. He hadn't seen Jim at all for most of the trip, but last night Jim had appeared in the corridor, said hello with a grin, and then added, "Just pretend the ocean is a big cornfield, and it won't be so scary," before walking off, too fast for Frankie to think of a suitable reply.

Restless, he set off for another stroll through the corridors, hoping to stumble on a poker game he could join. He did find one being conducted on a life raft, but suddenly decided maybe he wouldn't play after all. All those guys had looked like cardsharps anyway. It wasn't until he got to Deck Seven and found Jim curled up in a corner, trying to take a nap, that he realized he'd been looking for Jim all along. The thought gave him pause, but he ignored the flicker of apprehension, the sense that getting close to Jim could be dangerous.

Folding his long legs, he dropped onto the deck. Jim cracked open an eye and then sat up a little straighter. "Frankie. What are you doing here?"

"I just wanted to inform you that I am *not* afraid of the ocean. And we don't grow much corn in Idaho, you know. Least not where I'm from."

Jim stretched, his shirt riding up and exposing a strip of skin, dark hair smattered around his navel. "Let's say I believe this Idaho nonsense. What do you have instead of corn?"

"Well, we raise sheep on our ranch, along with alfalfa along the river. And of course there are potatoes on some farms. Lots of potatoes."

"I knew that. I've seen the bags in the grocery store." Jim yawned and leaned back against the wall, watching Frankie. "So, what? You ride horses and have sheepdogs and all that?"

"Yep. It's tough work, though. You're up early every morning, even in the winter when there's two feet of snow on the ground."

Jim made a face. "I've never lived somewhere it snowed. Don't want to, neither."

"Have you ever even seen snow?"

"Yes. I went on a trip once to the Sierras to go skiing in the winter."

"And?"

Jim chuckled. "I spent most of the time on my ass—couldn't manage those skis to save my life. So I got pretty well acquainted with the snow."

Frankie laughed, too, and then leaned over and nudged Jim's leg. "You'd like tobogganing, though, I bet. That's what we do in the winter for fun. There's this big hill without too many trees about a quarter mile from the house where we make a huge sled run. And then you get to eat stacks of buckwheat pancakes and bacon afterwards."

"Now that last part I could handle. Makes me hungry just thinking about it." Jim felt around in one of his pockets and drew out a battered Milky Way. "Want some?"

"Just a little piece."

Jim broke off an end, and Frankie popped it in his mouth. "You must have a real sweet tooth. I never see you but you're eating a candy bar."

"Guilty as charged." Jim licked the chocolate off his fingers. He had thick fingers, calloused from work, many of the nails broken off. Competent hands, Frankie thought, and then realized he was staring. He looked away, picking at a loose thread in his trousers.

"So have you lived in California your whole life?" he asked.

"Nah. We started off in Nevada. My dad had a job in a mine there. But after he got killed in an accident, my brother and I got sent to our uncle's in LA, like I told you. My mom had died years before."

"Sorry," Frankie muttered, feeling awkward.

Jim shrugged. "I don't remember my mom, really. I was only three when it happened. And I never liked my dad. Don't care too much for my uncle, either, but what can you do?"

Frankie thought of his own family and was glad they got along pretty well. Although what they'd do if he told them he was queer, he couldn't guess. He thought his mother might come to accept it, maybe, but not his dad. And Helen might not want him around her kids anymore.

"Why the long face?" Jim demanded.

"Nothing." Frankie stretched out his legs, sighing. "You got anything to do? Cards? Dice?"

Jim raised his eyebrows. "So it's my job to entertain you now too?" he asked, but didn't sound really upset. "Come on. I'll see what I can dig up."

Jim bunked in what looked like a converted utility closet. Grimacing, he wedged his hand in behind the stacked cots and managed to pull out his duffel bag. The contents did not prove very promising, however, and they finally ended up flipping Jim's pocket knife and seeing if they could get it to stick in the deck boards.

Frankie watched as Jim tossed it and the handle thumped into the floor for the tenth time. "Used to be better at this," Jim muttered.

On his turn, Frankie didn't have any more luck. "Guess it's a good thing they give us guns instead of knives."

They were sitting close enough that their boots touched, and Jim kept tapping his against Frankie's. "Is that Morse code or something?" Frankie asked.

Jim smiled. "Nah. I'm just antsy from being cooped up on this boat. Should be in port tomorrow, though."

Frankie nodded. "I can't wait to get back in a plane."

"You're not getting in anything until I've had a chance to look it over. I have to make sure it's in good shape before you start messing it up."

"Fine, but make it quick, would you? I hate being stuck on the ground."

Jim's mouth tilted in a smile. "I know. I've started to think that maybe you're part bird. A stork."

"A stork?"

"Those long legs of yours? Couldn't be anything else."

Laughing, Jim ducked away as Frankie tried to get him in a headlock.

THEY DID arrive in port as scheduled the next day. It was cloudy and rainy, and everyone got drenched as they stood around waiting for transports. It was another two hours by truck to the airbase that would be their squadron's home for the foreseeable future. Frankie watched the soft green fields and stone walls of the English countryside roll by outside the window. There were signs of war, though. One field had the remains of a Spitfire still crumpled in the dirt, and one little town had been shattered by bombs, probably dropped by mistake given that London or an airbase was a far more likely target.

When Frankie hopped off the truck at RAF Fowlmere, he immediately landed in a puddle about two inches deep. Cursing, he stepped out of it into equally deep mud. Lowering clouds hung just above the tree tops, and he was grateful for the rain slicker someone handed him. Fowlmere had been an RAF fighter station but had now been given over to the Eighth Air Force to house the 339th Fighter Group. Rows of Nissen huts dotted the green fields, their metal exteriors dull under the cloudy sky. Frankie trudged after Ed to the ones assigned to their own squadron. Inside their hut they found beds for fourteen men, a coke-burning stove, and not much else.

"Cheerful," Frankie commented, looking around.

"At least it's dry," Ed replied, choosing a bunk and tossing his bag onto it. "What do you think the odds are of getting a hot meal?"

"Slim to none?" Frankie hazarded. "It's only 1530."

Ed nodded gloomily. Frankie joined him at the window, and they looked out at the base. A small building directly adjacent to the barracks must be the showers and toilets. He suspected the pilot's lounge was the Nissen hut with the crowd at the door. Farther off, he could make out the runways—a P-47 was just taxiing to a halt—with the ready room to one side.

The sight made his stomach jumpy. The whole drive in, they'd been peppered with reports about the Allies' progress in France. Three weeks into the invasion, and it sounded like the initial fast advance had run into a brick wall. When the weather held, bombing runs were being sent to target anything that helped the Germans move their troops, as well as fighter bases and factories. They could get sent to escort the bombers or to run bombing and strafing missions of their own. Already he'd been treated to a graphic tale by a pilot in a squadron that had been here for three months. It had involved a greenhorn like himself getting bounced by an Fw 190 and shot out of the sky before he'd even known what was going on.

His first few runs, he would be the wingman for the flight leader. Two of the four planes in a flight were the attackers while the wingmen protected their backs. Of course, that left the wingman pretty open. The worst spot was Tail-End Charlie, stuck in the rear of the formation. Tail-End Charlies always got the worst of it.

Frankie knew the pilot had just been having some fun teasing the new arrivals, but he didn't doubt the story was true, either.

THEIR PLANES didn't arrive until two days later. In the meantime Frankie got to know the pilot's lounge and the local pub extremely well. If they wanted to go to the pub, they had to use bicycles, which made for a pretty interesting time coming back when they were all smashed. Roy went into a ditch twice, and Frankie almost tumbled straight over the handlebars. Now that their squadron was all together, he spent more time with Ed, Roy, and George again. Jim was busy, anyway. There were always things that needed fixing around a base, and he was preparing for the arrival of the P-51s and complaining about all the parts they didn't have yet. When the planes did come, Frankie went out to check on his as soon as possible and found Jim already there along with the rest of his aircrew, clambering over the Mustang and peering critically at screws.

"How does she look?" Frankie asked.

A few muttered grunts were all he got in reply.

"That bad?"

Jim heaved a dramatic sigh and slid off the wing onto the ground. "Everything *looks* fine. It's when you get it up into the air that the problems inevitably start. Damn factories have no idea what stresses actually get put on these things."

Frankie gave him a wry grin. "Gosh, that makes me feel so much better."

Jim clapped him on the shoulder. "Not to worry. We have our own tricks. She'll be ready and raring to go by your first mission."

Henry, his armorer, asked, "What are you going to call her? I know a guy who's a great artist. He could paint something on the nose."

Most of the guys named them after girlfriends or wives, of course. That was out in Frankie's case. So he said, "Dreamin' Dorothy."

Jim made a strangled noise, trying to keep a straight face.

"She your girlfriend?" Henry asked.

"Not quite," Frankie replied, mouth twitching.

Jim broke first, guffawing loudly.

Frankie gave him a little shove. "Figured I might as well stop trying to fight it."

Jim snickered some more and then clapped his hands. "I've got it—a pair of ruby slippers painted right on the nose." He reached up and patted the underside of the Mustang.

Frankie made a face. "Uh, no."

"Or a flying monkey," Henry offered, catching on to the joke.

"*Definitely* not." Frankie shook his head and glared at Jim. "If I come out here tomorrow and find a pair of shoes painted on the nose, just remember, I know where you sleep, and I'm not above using that knowledge."

Jim held up his hands. "I wouldn't think of it."

"You were just thinking of it. Don't lie," Frankie told him, and Jim laughed again.

CHAPTER ELEVEN

EVERYONE IN the squadron wanted to rush off to their first mission immediately, but they had to log several hours of training before they were moved to active status. An experienced pilot got to babysit them through it. His name was Mel Browning, and Frankie thought he looked tired and stressed.

"I hear he had to bail out after getting hit by flak over Bremen," Roy said out of the side of his mouth as they listened to Browning give them a lecture on paying attention to their coolant temperature gauge. The Mustang had maneuverability and range, but the coolant system was delicate. A direct hit to it and you were done for. It was either attempt a belly landing in a field somewhere or bail out.

"Guess they wanted to give him a break from combat," Frankie replied. "Although I'm not sure I'd call flying with us much of a break. One of the guys from the 504th was telling me that there's a place called the Flak Home just outside of Exeter. A nice, quiet spot in the country where you can go play tennis, read, sleep, or whatever."

Roy scoffed. "I just want to get a two-day pass up to London. That's all the relaxation I'll need."

The training flights were pretty boring, although a few mock dogfights broke out. Some days they saw streams of bombers and fighters headed toward Germany. Oftentimes, though, potential missions got scrubbed due to the weather. Fog, clouds, rain, you name it, and Britain had it. When the clouds got really thick, they would have to rely on instruments only. It had hardly ever been cloudy back in Arizona or at Merced during their transition training—certainly never this all-encompassing fog—but sometimes they had been put into flight simulators, usually a Link Trainer with a wooden hood covering it so they could only use their instruments. Actually flying without your eyes, though, well, Frankie hoped that their first mission wouldn't be like that.

Every morning before he went up, he visited Jim to see how the plane checked out. He called it visiting at any rate; Jim called it "pestering."

"Go away," Jim would say. "I'm trying to work. Go eat breakfast."

"I ate breakfast," Frankie would reply. "Want some coffee?" He had started bringing a thermos of coffee to Jim, who often looked sleepy at such an early hour. Jim had once confided that if he had his way, he would never get out of bed until nine at the earliest.

"If I take it, will you leave?" Jim would ask.

"I'll go sit over there and be real quiet," Frankie would reply, gesturing at the nearest pile of crates. Jim would grudgingly take the thermos and shoo Frankie away, usually stuffing his rain slicker into Frankie's arms because Frankie always forgot to bring his despite the perpetual drizzle. "Wear it," Jim would say and then mutter something about how he was doomed to take care of absentminded pilots, and who had made Frankie a pilot in the first place, anyway, if he couldn't even remember his damn raincoat?

This morning, though, their required hours of training flights had been logged, and they had been cleared to fly a mission. Frankie had hardly been able to sleep, stomach jumping with nerves, and he was awake already when the orderly came in at 0330 with word that the mission was a go, and they were to report to the briefing room in an hour.

He didn't even need coffee that morning, adrenaline keeping him alert. The lights in the briefing room were too harsh for the early hour, and he could easily tell who the old hands were, slouching in their chairs and yawning. The new pilots tried to look casual but couldn't quite manage it. Frankie kept drumming his pen on his knee. The briefing officer informed them they would be escorting a group of bombers to Hamburg, enemy aircraft a possibility, certainly anti-aircraft fire. At the end of the briefing, they did the time hack, all setting their watches to the same minute.

Frankie's heart was racing, the underarms of his shirt already damp with sweat when he climbed into his plane. He had on all his gear—Mae West, oxygen mask, dinghy, knife, sidearm, survival kit—and it was a job squeezing into the seat. Then Jim was there, helping him to get settled.

"Don't get distracted by any cows, okay?" Jim said.

"What does that even mean?" Frankie demanded, giving him an exasperated glare.

"It means don't do anything bonkers. Just stay in position and try not to get shot."

"Do I tell you how to fix the plane?" Frankie grumbled, but then he gave Jim a quick grin. "And I'll be fine, knucklehead. You're not getting rid of me so easy."

Jim slapped his shoulder, gave Frankie's helmet his customary knock, and then jumped down.

Frankie pulled the canopy shut, nerves soaring again now that Jim was no longer distracting him.

The air was alive with the rumble of engines with all three squadrons based at Fowlmere participating in the mission. The planes started slipping into the sky, one after the other, more taking their place on the runway as soon as a space was clear. Frankie rolled into position and soon could gun the throttle, the Mustang dipping slightly as it left the ground and then soaring upward. He maneuvered into position, right behind the wing leader of Green Flight.

At first everything seemed to be going as planned. But as they drew near the Channel, more and more clouds began building. His sight vanished entirely a few miles later, subsumed into a murky sea of fog. Then the call came over the radio: "All flights, this is squadron leader. The mission has been scrubbed. Return to base."

It was tricky, getting everyone turned about safely in all the clouds. Collisions could happen so easily in these conditions. The week before they'd arrived at Fowlmere, two planes had run into each other in a thick bank of clouds, killing both pilots. But this time they all made it safely, trailing the leading edge of fog as they landed.

As he taxied in, Jim was waiting by a truck, peering intently at Frankie's plane.

"No damage," Frankie told him when he climbed out. "As you probably guessed, we didn't make it far. Fucking weather." He scowled.

"I figured. Didn't Foggy Belmont say it was going to be nice and clear?"

"Yeah, well, even the weather officer gets it wrong sometimes. It probably won't clear enough to reschedule the mission, either." Frankie sagged against the side of the plane. "Damn. I'm exhausted and we didn't even *do* anything." The tension from earlier had melted away, leaving him drained. But he would have to go through the exact same thing tomorrow, if the weather improved and a mission got scheduled.

"Give me a chance to get the plane checked out, and then I'll let you beat me in Ping-Pong," Jim said. "That'll make you feel better."

"You won't *let* me beat you," Frankie corrected. "I'll beat you whether you're letting me or not."

"Just keep on telling yourself that." Jim gave him a shove toward the ready room. "Now go. Have some coffee. Or tea—isn't that what all the Brits drink? Stop pestering me."

"All right, all right." Frankie wandered off and ended up in the pilot's lounge, drinking coffee, not tea, and reading a letter from his mother.

David is still somewhere in the Pacific, his mother tells me. She's so afraid, Frankie, and she's almost become resigned to bad news. I'm not resigned—never will be resigned. I know you'll be coming home to us. Your father spends every night listening to the radio and criticizing Patton's decisions (and God help us when he gets started on Churchill). We have an atlas always open on the coffee table, and your brother plots imaginary missions for you in France and Germany. I suppose

*if one good thing is going to come from this war, it's
that Colin will get an A in geography! Your sisters
send their good wishes—all of us do.*

Frankie scrubbed a hand over his face and took another swig
of coffee to drown the sudden pang of homesickness. So David
was still in the Pacific where the infantry was slugging it out with
the Japs, one island at a time. *Please, God, keep him safe.* Maybe
David didn't want his prayers anymore, but that was too damn bad.
Frankie couldn't just give up on him like that, even if David had
given up on him.

Jim found him there, sitting on a stool and feeling sorry for
himself. He dragged Frankie over to the Ping-Pong table and shoved
the paddle into his hand despite his protests that he was too tired.

"You need something to take your mind off stuff," Jim replied.
"I'm not letting you get into my plane all coiled up in a ball of
tension. You'll do something stupid and blame it on the wiring. You
do know that I'm going for the record of least number of missions
aborted on account of mechanical failures, right?"

Frankie rolled his eyes. "I'd hate to get in the way of your
lofty aims."

"No shit. I'm going to keep those spark plugs so clean you
could wipe your ass with them."

It made Frankie laugh, and he tossed up the ball and served.
Jim grinned back at him, even as he darted for it.

It was a close game, but Frankie felt better, even if he did
squeak by with the win. He felt like he might be able to get some
sleep tonight.

"I think they're showing *Coney Island* in the mess hall after
dinner," Jim said when they had surrendered their paddles to the
next two guys waiting to play. "Want to go see it? George
Montgomery and Betty Grable. Plenty of singing."

"Nah, I'll pass. I'm going to write some letters, have an early
night."

Jim nodded slowly, brown eyes intent on Frankie's face. Then
he shrugged and turned to go. "See you tomorrow, then."

As he left, Frankie almost changed his mind and called him back. He liked Jim, liked him a lot. Probably too much, and that was what made him let Jim keep walking. If he slipped up, Jim might realize how he felt. It had happened so gradually, their initial animosity melting into friendlier teasing, and finally a genuine liking of each other's company. He was determined not to let himself ruin that and tried his damnedest to keep his thoughts from wandering. Jim's muscular arms, dark brown eyes, and calloused hands would be enough to fuel plenty of fantasies, but he valued Jim's friendship too much to lose it.

AN ORDERLY woke him at 0330 again the next morning, rousing him from a fitful sleep. "There's a mission scheduled, sir. Briefing at five."

The last clinging shreds of sleep dissolved. Frankie lay there a moment, the chilly air making his nose cold, trying not to tense up too much. The weather had to be clear. It just had to. He couldn't go through this every morning. Despite being tired the evening before, he had started feeling nervous once he went to bed. He'd woken up what seemed like every half hour, too wired to sleep well. If he could just get this first time over with, and hopefully survive to fly more missions, then maybe it wouldn't be so bad in the future.

When they all clattered into the briefing room a few minutes before five, the sky had turned a pale bluish-gray, free of clouds. Everyone's eyes immediately went to the curtain that covered the map at the front of the room. Finally an officer pulled it aside. A red string went from England to a black dot in Germany. Frankie squinted. It was Hanover.

"Thank fuck," Roy muttered. "I was sure it was going to be Berlin."

"You'll be flying an escort mission today, boys," the CO said. "Three boxes of bombers aiming for an industrial complex." He gave the rendezvous coordinates and Frankie, like the rest of the pilots, wrote them on the back of his hand.

Frankie was going to be part of Blue Flight—Blue Two more specifically. Their flight leader was Ben Lawson, who had been here since early May. Frankie would be his wingman.

"Just stick right on my ass," he told Frankie with a grin. "And don't mind the flak."

Frankie mustered a weak smile in return. He fumbled for a stick of gum to ease the dryness in his mouth.

Outside on the runway, the sun seemed unusually bright after so many cloudy days. His flight jacket was a heavy weight, too hot with its fleece lining, but he knew once they were up to 12,000 feet, he'd be grateful for it.

Jim met him at the plane. "Heard you're heading for Hanover," he said, clambering up behind Frankie and helping him get situated.

"Yep." Frankie looked up at him, shading his eyes. "See you in a few hours, I guess."

Jim opened his mouth to say something and then paused.

"What?" Frankie asked.

Jim gave a quick shake of his head. "Our Mustang won't give you any trouble. She's running like a dream."

"Oh, so it's *ours* now, is it?" Frankie grinned. "Finally ready to admit I'm a swell pilot, huh?"

Jim snorted. "Nah. I just figured it would give you more incentive to help me clean the landing gear struts." He knocked his fist on Frankie's helmet. "See you 'round, Dorothy."

Frankie was still smiling as he ran through his preflight check. Jim might claim it wasn't true, but he knew Jim would only grant dual ownership of a plane to someone he thought was a good pilot. It surprised him how much Jim's good opinion meant to him.

Up in the air, he swung in behind Lawson, and soon the familiar stillness of high altitude flying settled over them. No sounds beyond the steady rumble of the Merlin engine and the swish of his breath through the oxygen mask. He listened intently to the engine. The Mustang liked to give a slight shudder if the engine was about to stall. Not that he didn't believe Jim, but staying alert kept you alive. He also kept scanning the skies, even if he knew they were really too far away for any German fighters to be hovering around, waiting to pounce.

When he wasn't watching the skies, he tracked their progress on the ground. The green fields and towns of England gave way to the forbidding waters of the Channel. Frankie had to double-check to make sure he was wearing his Mae West. The last thing he wanted was to bail out over the water and be without a life vest. Even with one, you had to pray the rescue boats would spot you in time. The water was too cold to survive in it for long.

Then suddenly the water disappeared, replaced by the shores of the Netherlands.

Frankie's adrenaline shot up another notch. He wished he could do a barrel roll, just to let off some steam, but none of them could break formation. Pestering Roy over the radio was also out. Not only would everyone else in the squadron hear, but Lawson would yell at him for it. The radio was only for critical communications.

For the first time, Frankie wished he had been transferred to twin-engines, because at least in a bomber, you'd have other people to talk to during a long flight.

Then he remembered that he wasn't alone, not really. His Mustang hummed around him, engine purring contentedly. "Impatient to get there?" he murmured. "Me too. I know we haven't been acquainted for long, but we'll see each other through this."

He imagined that the black-and-yellow checkerboard markings that decorated the nose gleamed a little brighter, contrasting with the dark green that extended up to the canopy and out onto the wings.

"Just promise me you won't go into a stall, okay?" He trusted Jim and the rest of his aircrew, but a lot of pilots complained about the Mustang's finicky nature, particularly those who had flown Jugs, the P-47s. The Jugs didn't have the same maneuverability, but they could take anything that was thrown at them.

Frankie had gotten into quite the heated argument with a guy in the pilot's lounge a few days ago, in fact, over the merits of the P-51 compared to earlier models. He had defended his Mustang's beautiful responsiveness and its speed, backed up by George and

Ed. But loving his plane didn't mean he was blind to its—few—faults.

The Merlin engine thrummed a bit louder, as though saying it would never dream of failing Frankie when he needed it.

Grinning, he squeezed the stick in reply and tried to get his stomach to settle.

Twenty minutes later they spotted the bomber stream, right where it was supposed to be. Navigation was always a bit of a trick, with just a magnetic compass, the remote-reading compass indicator, and your watch to go by. Often they relied on calling a homing station on the radio to guide them back to base. But today they'd arrived right where they were supposed to be. The bomber stream looked like a dark cloud on the horizon at first, but as they drew closer, it separated into individual B-17s flying slowly but steadily toward the target. No sign of any bogies.

They moved into position above the bombers, Frankie craning his neck to watch the sky, squinting against the sunlight, which was growing brighter as a few clouds drifted away, little puffs of white against the expansive blue.

The flak started three minutes from the target. At the first explosion, he had to clench his muscles to avoid jerking the plane to the right. Thankfully, the fighters seemed to be high enough to avoid most of it, his plane only shuddering now and then from a shockwave. But the bombers down below were not so lucky. Black smoke blossomed in their midst, fading away only for another burst to materialize. As the missiles shot upward from the ground, they trailed streams of red, green, and yellow smoke. It reminded Frankie of shooting off fireworks on the Fourth of July.

They couldn't do anything about flak. Frankie could only watch as one of the bombers started listing sideways, fire licking its way up from an engine. Then the tail broke off, like some giant hand had reached out to snap it in two. The bomber went into a nosedive. A few seconds later, white parachutes came into view as the crew bailed out.

Three more bombers got hit before it was time to release their loads. Another one went down, but the other two started running back to base, and Frankie prayed they would make it. He thought of Pete, now a navigator on a bomber. Last he'd heard, Pete was being sent to the Pacific, just like David.

Although duty kept his eyes on the sky, he couldn't resist taking quick peeks down at the ground to see the bombs explode. The Air Forces tried to hit military targets; that's why they were out here in the daylight, to give the bombardiers a better chance of accuracy, unlike the Brits who bombed under the cover of night. Frankie couldn't really blame them, though. They'd suffered through the Blitz, large chunks of London reduced to rubble. That might change his perspective on the matter too.

By God, but they were lucky to have an entire ocean in between America and the Axis. So far, the Japs had managed the only big hit, and that hadn't been anywhere near the mainland.

The bomber stream turned in a wide loop, doing one more pass over the target before heading for home. Still no sign of fighters, and Frankie cursed. A milk run, that's what it was going to be. Then he thought of the bombers that had gone down and felt a stab of guilt. It hadn't been a milk run for everybody.

The trip back was just as long and silent as the way out. Coming into base, the tension slowly trickled out of him, leaving him weak and shaky. After he taxied to a halt, he sat there for a second, ears adjusting to the quiet after the constant sound of the engine. Then he forced himself to move, popping the top and hopping out.

Jim was waiting for him, a critical eye on the plane. "Well?" he asked.

"A milk run," Frankie said. "Didn't see one damn thing to shoot at. On the plus side, the engine didn't stall."

"Of course it didn't," Jim retorted, although he sounded kind of distracted, and his eyes lingered on Frankie's face before snapping away.

Frankie still felt a bit unsettled, and he ducked under the P-51, moving to the other side so he could watch the rest of the squadron land. The field was alive with movement—trucks rumbling past, men shouting, and the drone of engines. A brisk wind had come up, chilling his sweaty flight suit, but he took a deep breath just the same, the stench of gasoline almost drowned out by the smell of wet grass.

Jim came to stand next to him. Frankie glanced over, but Jim didn't say anything, so Frankie turned his attention back to the hustle and bustle of the airfield. This was better. This hurry of life and relief and clean air. Better than the long silence of the flight, sticking to the tight formation, and that bomber breaking apart like a balsa-wood model.

A pressure on his wrist made him look down to see two of Jim's fingers resting there.

Frankie's heart started thudding faster.

Slowly Jim moved his thumb to join them, giving Frankie's wrist a light caress.

Was this... was Jim doing what he thought he was doing? Possibilities swirled through his mind. It might be a joke. Maybe he should laugh and shove Jim away. Or it might *not* be a joke. And if not....

He let out a shaky breath and held still.

Jim smiled and turned his hand over, tracing his palm. Then he slung an arm around Frankie's shoulders and pulled him close, ruffling his hair and laughing when Frankie tried to wriggle out of his grip.

"I'm so goddamn keen on you," Jim whispered.

Frankie sucked in a breath and stilled, leaning back just a little into the solid, unyielding muscles of Jim's chest. Everything he had been thinking about a few seconds ago—the mission, the downed bomber—had been driven clean out of his head. "I—" he started.

"Frankie!"

Roy's voice punctured the little bubble of quiet that had briefly drawn around them. Footsteps clattered over the ground.

Frankie jerked away from Jim just as Roy rounded the nose of his plane, George on his heels, grinning.

"There you are! Come on, or did you forget Ed promised to treat us all in the pub if we made it back?" Roy grabbed his arm, and

George got around onto his other side, shoving. "We commandeered a Jeep. No fucking bicycles tonight. We're taking off right after the debriefing."

He couldn't refuse. What excuse could he possibly give for not wanting to celebrate their first mission?

"All right. Jeez—no need to yank off my arm, Roy." He looked over his shoulder. Jim wasn't even watching him anymore. He was talking to the armorer, gesturing at one of the machine guns.

A disorienting sense of doubt assailed him. Perhaps he had just imagined that whole thing with Jim. The adrenaline high playing a trick on his senses.

And then Jim glanced his way, and the corner of his mouth twitched into a smile. Relieved, Frankie grinned back—and promptly stumbled into a pothole because he wasn't watching where he was going.

Jim started laughing at him, the bastard, and Frankie gave him the finger. But he didn't stop smiling, either.

CHAPTER TWELVE

FOAM FLOATED on top of the beer and stuck to Frankie's upper lip. He scrubbed it away, pleasantly woozy after a couple of drinks.

"I can't believe I didn't realize it," he said to Ed, who was sitting next to him at the bar.

Ed raised his eyebrows. "Realize what? How sore your ass gets sitting in a plane for six hours?"

"No, that Jim—" He recollected himself just in time. Christ, he hadn't been able to think about anything else ever since they left the airfield. First he had been stuck on berating himself for never having approached Jim. He had been so worried about losing their friendship, so certain Jim would never return his feelings. Then his mind had rapidly gone through a list of topics ranging from whether Jim had ever been with anybody else, which he quickly decided must be a yes, to thinking about what Jim might have done with them and what he might be doing soon with Frankie. His brain had stuttered to a stop there because although Frankie had only his night with Sergio to go on, that didn't mean he didn't have an imagination.

"Well?" Ed prompted.

"Nothing." He could tell Ed, of course, but not in the middle of the pub and not when he wasn't even sure how this thing between him and Jim would turn out. "Just that I didn't realize how thankful I am my aircrew keeps my engine so nice and clean. Wouldn't have wanted to be in Henderson or Gregg's shoes—forced to turn back to base because of engine trouble."

"True. I think all of us are glad to have the first one behind us."

George had gone outside a few minutes ago to read a letter that had been waiting for him when they returned from the mission, and

Roy had followed. Those two would have kept poking and teasing, and maybe he would have let something incriminating slip. But Ed wouldn't push him, and he'd keep Frankie from doing anything too stupid.

"I'm glad we're all here in it together, Ed." Frankie waved a hand, trying to encompass the stodgy interior of the little pub, the thick accents of the locals rising in between the American twang of the pilots, the remembered bursts of flak and bombs. "It's all so strange sometimes, you know? It helps to be surrounded by familiar faces, I guess is what I'm trying to say."

"I know," Ed agreed, and he did seem to understand.

"Pete—you remember him, right? You know how I thought—sometimes I hoped—he would be there, in *that* way." Frankie took a long swallow. "And then he wasn't, but now I think, maybe, someone else might be." He motioned for another beer, but Ed stopped him.

"That's good, Frankie. Real good, but I think you've had enough, yeah? Chances are we'll be flying another mission tomorrow."

Frankie nodded and then grinned because he hadn't even been thinking about the next one. He'd been thinking about Jim. He remembered those two WASPs back in Arizona—Iris and Bonnie, and the way they'd been kissing, their easy, happy way with each other. Realizing maybe he could have that—it was a glorious, elated feeling that pushed every other sensation into the far recesses of his mind. He grabbed Ed's hand. "Pete, he couldn't ever—he had a fiancée, for Christ's sake, but Jim, he—"

"I get it." Ed grinned and shook his head. "I've felt that way myself a few times. But let's not talk about this right now," he added with a meaningful look at the pair of lieutenants sitting at the bar next to them. "We should get back to the base. George and Roy better not have taken that Jeep, because if you tried to ride a bike right now, you'd go straight into a ditch."

Frankie sighed but followed obediently. He started to open his mouth again when they got outside, but they were both brought up short by the sight of George standing by the Jeep, shoulders hunched, hands balled into fists. Roy stood by his side, holding a piece of paper.

"Hey, guys," Roy started to say, "George had some bad news—"

George cut in, his voice breaking the still evening like water drops sizzling on a hot griddle. "Those fuckers killed him. Those fucking Nazis killed my brother!"

He kicked the tire of the Jeep, a sharp, savage movement, and then banged his fists on the hood. "I'm going to kill *them*. I'm going to blow those fucking—oh *God*."

His sobs jerked his shoulders up and down.

Frankie's buzz faded, leaving him sick and mortified. He didn't look at Ed as they helped Roy get George into the Jeep. When they got back to the airfield, Frankie went to the barracks and flopped onto his bunk. The sick fascination that had gripped him when the flak hammered the skies around his plane, the dizzying joy sparked by Jim's words, the raw fury of George's grief—it all roiled inside him, finally settling into a hard ball pressing against his heart.

THE HEAVY tension was still there when he stumbled to the toilets in the dark to take a piss and splash some water on his face. He brushed his teeth, too, scrubbing away the sour taste of alcohol.

When he emerged, Jim was waiting for him.

"Christ!" Frankie glared. "You practically gave me a heart attack, jumping out of the dark like that."

Jim grabbed his arm and dragged him away from the dim light illuminating the door to the toilets. "I've been freezing my ass off for the last hour, waiting for you. Where the hell have you been?"

"George had bad news about his brother. Roy needed help getting him calmed down. And then, well, I couldn't just go wandering around looking for you."

"Because a pilot couldn't possibly have a reason to speak to his aircrew chief." Jim snorted. "That mouth of yours made me forget how dumb you can be."

Frankie should have been annoyed—he *was* annoyed. But—
"My mouth, huh?" he asked, surprised at how low and rough his
voice sounded.

"Yeah, your fucking mouth. Spouting off such irritating
nonsense all the time when obviously it should be doing other
things." Jim had drawn closer, near enough that the toe of his boot
hit Frankie's.

Frankie gave it a gentle kick. "What other things?"

"Oh, I think you can guess." He knew Jim was smiling, even
though it was hard to make out in the dark. "You're dumb but not
that dumb."

He should make some retort, but instead he was reaching out,
finding Jim's hand, hardly able to breathe for fear it would be
snatched away.

Jim curled his fingers around Frankie's, warm and firm. "This
okay?" he whispered, leaning closer, stretching up on his toes a
little.

"Yeah." Frankie tilted his head and met Jim's kiss.

Jim started off a little to the edge of Frankie's mouth and then
moved to the center. Frankie had thought it would be rough, but
instead Jim was surprisingly gentle and slow. Winding an arm under
Jim's, Frankie clutched at his shoulder and kissed back eagerly. Jim
made an approving noise in his throat.

When they parted, Frankie kept his head bent, Jim's hair
brushing against his forehead.

"How long have you wanted to do this?" Frankie asked,
keeping his voice soft.

He felt Jim shrug. "Not sure. You annoyed the shit out of me
at first. And then I started thinking about how you'd look on your
knees. You wouldn't be able to say anything with my dick in your
mouth."

Frankie shivered, arousal simmering in his gut.

"And then... well, I guess you just kind of grew on me. I
promised myself if you got back from your first mission alive, I
would tell you." Jim huffed a short laugh. "I still wasn't quite sure if
I had pegged you right. I thought I had, but I wasn't sure."

Frankie blushed, glad Jim couldn't see it as he confessed, "I never even guessed that you felt that way. About me or any guy."

"It's not something you can have the whole world knowing, is it?"

"No." Frankie paused, thinking. "Wait, the night you took me to that bar—was that a date?"

Jim's laugh tickled Frankie's ear. "Maybe."

"Well, it was an awful one, just for the record."

"I'll have to see if I can do better, then." One of his hands was starting to slip down Frankie's back toward his ass when footsteps and voices jerked them apart again.

"Fuck," Jim muttered. He held still a moment, listening.

Frankie groped toward him again, but Jim had already stepped back. "Meet me here tomorrow night at nine," he ordered. "We'll have to make it quick."

"That's okay. Quick is okay." Anything would be okay as long as it meant getting Jim's hands back on him.

Jim laughed again and strode off, leaving Frankie to take some cooling breaths and get a handle on himself before returning to his bunk. Once everyone else had turned in for the night, though, he shoved a hand into his shorts and brought himself off to the memory of Jim's mouth on his.

UNFORTUNATELY, THE war didn't stop overnight, and they got called out for a mission, meaning the fantasies Frankie had been indulging in of dragging Jim off to some isolated corner of the base would indeed have to wait until evening, as Jim had promised.

Adjusting his oxygen mask and regretting that third cup of coffee, Frankie flicked his eyes between his instruments. He could see Blue Leader in front of him, the tail of Lawson's P-51 a reassuring landmark in the sea of hazy clouds. The rest of the flight was invisible, swallowed up in the murk. Foggy Belmont had assured them the weather would be clear over their target, though, even if they had to rely on instrument flying most of the way there.

Not that everyone believed him. "It's women and children weather," one of the pilots had said as they huddled in the ready room around the stove. That meant there was a good chance the bombers would miss the target and hit civilians instead.

But there was no point thinking about it—nothing he could do. And so Frankie allowed his thoughts to return to two hours before, when he was preparing to take off. Jim, as always, had helped him get settled in the cockpit. What was new was the way his touch set off a thrum of arousal in Frankie that he didn't have to ignore, only try hard to tamp down. Jim had knocked on his helmet. "Don't get lost, Dorothy," he had said, grinning like he knew exactly the effect he was having. Then he had leaned closer and whispered, "Extra incentive to get home today, huh?"

"Ah, goddammit, Jim!" Frankie had shouted after him, drawing confused expressions from Henry and the rest of the aircrew. It had taken until halfway over the Channel for his trousers to feel less uncomfortably tight.

Their target that day was a ball-bearing factory in Schweinfurt. Resistance was expected to be heavy. Reports from the advancing troops in France had the Ninth Corps moving toward Cherbourg, while the Brits and Canadians tried to eliminate the Germans dug in around Caen. The Air Forces had dedicated themselves to weakening the Germans' lines of supply, softening up the resistance that land forces were encountering. Frankie had written "Maybe Berlin by the end of the summer!" in the last letter he'd sent to his mother.

That might have been stretching the mark a bit, though, he admitted to himself as the cloud cover started to dissipate. He pulled back his glove to check the coordinates he'd written on his hand during their briefing. They were coming up on their expected rendezvous point with the bombers, and the Jerries might appear at any moment.

Even though it would be hell for the bomber crews if they did—and not a day went by that Frankie didn't thank God he wasn't stuck in a B-17, with no choice but to keep flying steadily toward the target no matter what came at you—Frankie and the rest of the guys in the squadron were itching to get into some dogfights. Sure, it was unlikely he would get a kill as long as he was covering Lawson, but he might get off a few shots nonetheless.

"Worst thing would be if the war ends before we get to shoot anything," Roy had declared gloomily the other day. "All those months of training for nothing."

And now George was hell-bent on revenge for his brother.

"Don't let it get to your head," Ed had warned him that morning as they came out of the briefing. "Stay in formation."

George had nodded, but his lips had been pressed in a grim line, red hair outlining his pale face.

Frankie was just checking his coolant temperature gauge—the Mustang had a nasty habit of overheating if the automatic system malfunctioned—when the call came crackling over the radio.

"Bogies at one o'clock high!"

A second later he caught sight of the bomber box. A swarm of Me 109s were climbing up to attack them from below. Craning his neck up to the right, Frankie spotted the other threat—several flights of Messerschmitts, the Me 109s, and Fock-Wulfs, the Fw 190s, diving down at the fighter squadron. They'd have to leave the bombers on their own for the moment or they'd never make it there, not with all these fighters on their tail.

Heart hammering in his throat, Frankie kept his eyes on Lawson, staying right behind him. One second, the German fighters appeared small and distant up against the sun. Then an Me 109 started growing bigger with alarming speed, coming right for them. Lawson broke off to the right and angled upward to meet it, getting off a few squirts. The 109 performed a split-S to the deck. Lawson didn't follow, intent on making it to the bombers. A quick glance showed they were being pounded. A B-17 at the back of the stream fell into a steep dive even as Frankie watched, smoke pouring out. No sign of any parachutes.

As he and Lawson curved back around, a 109 tumbled past with its tail section on fire, almost shearing through Frankie's right wing.

"Shit!" Frankie couldn't help jerking sideways, losing his position for a moment. As he drew back into formation, a P-51 darted past, following the wounded 109. The numbers on the tail proclaimed the Mustang to be George.

George fired his guns steadily at the burning 109. Its cockpit flipped off and the German pilot tumbled out, his parachute flowering into a white cloud.

Instead of breaking off, George turned his guns on the pilot.

"Oh fuck," Frankie breathed, unable to look away.

The parachute shredded like paper. The pilot's body jerked a few times, and then he was gone, falling out of view.

A chill shuddered through Frankie. But he didn't have time to dwell on it, because they were coming up on the bombers now, and Lawson had slipped in behind an Fw 190 that didn't realize they were there, intent on the B-17 in its sights.

Lawson let off a few squirts, and when he broke off, Frankie shot a few bursts, too, although the 190 looked pretty battered already. The rattle of the guns vibrated through his body, jarring his teeth. The starboard gun suddenly cut off. It must have jammed.

They roared past the B-17, close enough that Frankie caught a glimpse of the ball turret gunner, curled up in his bubble, face twisted into a yell as he swiveled his guns toward another Jerry.

By the time they circled around, the Luftwaffe had pulled away, leaving the air empty and still beneath the thrumming roar of the engines. They would be waiting for them on the way back, though. For the first time since he had started flying, he wanted to land before a flight was over. His emotions were all over the place, and he longed to stop the plane and just sit quietly for a few minutes to get a hold of himself. But they had to keep going. The flak would start up as soon as they drew near the target, dark clouds whose trajectory you couldn't predict. And in the back of his mind, the memory of that shredded parachute hovered, wanting to push everything else aside and surge to the fore in all its sick horror.

Gripping the stick, he tried to blank it all away and think of nothing but the formation and the quivering needle on his airspeed indicator.

The fighters flew high enough that the flak wasn't too much of a threat. But he watched four more bombers succumb, falling away toward the ground, swallowed up by the clouds of smoke billowing up from where the bombs were exploding.

They got pounced again by the Jerries on the way back, just as he had expected. This time he and Lawson didn't get anything— only a few squirts at a 109 that quickly broke off, executing a neat turn and dive. Even with their auxiliary tank, they didn't have enough fuel for extended dogfights, and Lawson kept their pursuits to a minimum. They headed back into the clouds, a gray world enshrouding them. It was as though they had been transported into some hellish dimension and now were transitioning back into reality.

When he finally taxied to a halt at Fowlmere, Frankie undid his straps and then just sat slumped in the seat. His limbs felt like rubber, and he wasn't at all sure his legs would hold him when he jumped out.

A hiss of air signaled the opening of the canopy. He blinked up into Jim's face.

"You planning on sleeping there?" Jim asked, but his hand lingered a few seconds after clapping Frankie on the shoulder.

His voice didn't work right at first, but finally he said, "No," and hauled himself out, sagging against one of the wheel struts. He watched as Jim climbed onto one of the wings.

Tonight, Jim had promised. Frankie's eyes slid partway closed, his mind wandering from the image of Jim crouched on the wing to one of Jim pressed flush against him, mouth open, hands jerking at Frankie's trousers. He let his eyes shut.

As soon as he did, the white parachute was there, the pilot jerking as the bullets sliced into him.

Frankie wrenched his head up. He focused again on Jim, making sure to keep his eyes open.

"Hey, Frankie!" It was Roy, waving his arm, helmet dangling from his fingers. "Come on. We have a debriefing to get to."

Frankie lurched into motion with a sigh, giving Jim a wave. Jim tapped the watch on his wrist, a silent "See you later."

"You seen Ed?" Roy asked as Frankie joined him.

"No." Frankie rolled his shoulders, sore from so long in the cockpit.

"I was *this* close to getting a hit on a Messerschmitt," Roy continued. "Damn thing turned left at the last second. George won't shut up about his score, of course."

Frankie felt a burst of anger. "He didn't have to take out the pilot."

Roy looked surprised at his vehement tone. "Maybe not, but you know the Jerries never rotate their pilots out. If George hadn't done it, that pilot would have been flying again in a couple of days. And maybe this time he'd have killed someone *you* care about."

"I know... I wasn't...." Frankie stopped, scrubbing a hand through his hair. "I get why George did it. I just...." He trailed off and shrugged, unable to voice what he meant, wishing he hadn't said anything.

There was no sign of Ed at the debriefing. George sat down next to Frankie and Roy, and he gave Frankie a look, like he didn't want to brag but was waiting for Frankie to acknowledge what he'd done.

"Guess you're the first of us to draw blood," Frankie told him, mustering up a grin and slapping his shoulder.

"Always was the best shot," George returned lightly. Then he fell quiet, leaning back in his chair. "Wake me when it starts, yeah?"

Frankie could have used a nap. But he kept fidgeting, eyes straying to the door. Where *was* Ed? It wasn't like him to miss a debriefing.

Ed never showed. They finally tracked down his flight leader and found out Ed had disappeared in the clouds on the return trip. Maybe he had gotten lost and disoriented but managed to land at a friendly base in France. Maybe he'd bailed out. Or maybe he'd nosedived into the ground, his plane crumpling up like a candy wrapper and crushing him. It had happened before to pilots when the clouds were thick and they thought down was up until it was too late.

A cold wave of shock rolled over Frankie. Ed couldn't be gone.

Roy lit a cigarette and offered one to Frankie. "Gotta happen to one of us sooner or later."

Frankie slowly took the cigarette and lit it, inhaling deeply. "Guess it did." It was stupid to think they would all make it through this unscathed. But how did one prepare for the death of a friend?

He didn't want to think about any of it. If he did—Christ, he might not be able to get back up in his plane tomorrow. So he kept busy—reading the news, playing some Ping-Pong, seeing if he could scrounge up a decent cup of coffee somewhere, and waiting. He counted off every hour until finally it was time, and he could go find Jim.

A light drizzle pattered on his head when he ducked outside. None of the others paid him any heed, absorbed in their card games, letters, and fiddling with the radio.

The blackout curtains kept the airfield dark and with the rain, there wasn't even a moon or stars to grant some light. Frankie fumbled his way to the back of the hut. He hesitated, peering into the blackness. "Jim?" he whispered.

A rustling noise, and then a hand touched his arm.

"So you came," Jim murmured. "Thought you might be too spooked."

"I'm not!" Frankie exclaimed indignantly. He put his own hand over Jim's. "It's just been a long day."

"What happened?" Jim asked, probably hearing the sorrow that strained Frankie's voice.

"I think we lost Ed. He is—he was—my friend."

Jim was silent for a moment. "I'm sorry."

"It's war, I know." Frankie heaved in a breath, angry at himself and the panic and fear that had gripped his heart ever since the mission, refusing to loosen its grip. He couldn't take these things so hard or he'd never make it.

"Still." Jim curled their fingers together. Slowly, he drew Frankie toward him. Frankie could just make out the angles of Jim's face, indistinct and blunt in the darkness. "If you don't want—"

"No, I do," Frankie said quickly. "Please."

Jim touched the side of his face first, smoothing his thumb along the rim of Frankie's ear, along his jaw, and then coming to rest on his mouth. Frankie flicked his tongue out, nervous.

Jim expelled a sharp breath, and gripping Frankie's shoulders, he drew closer. Frankie leaned in and kissed him. He twined his arms around Jim's back and fisted his right hand in Jim's shirt. God, he needed this. Something good, something that wasn't tinged with death.

Jim pressed forward, and Frankie stumbled backward, still growing used to the sensation of Jim's lips on his, of the rasp of stubble and the smell of the cheap soap they were issued, mingled with Jim's sweat. His back hit the end of the Nissen hut with a muffled clang.

"Shit," Frankie gasped, pulling away. Jim kept his hands on his shoulders, though, keeping him still. They waited, hearts thrumming.

All remained quiet. Frankie said a silent prayer of thanks. Then, tentative, he reached out, fumbling in the dark until he felt Jim's hair under his fingertips, damp from the rain. Jim allowed it, leaning into the caress.

He kissed Frankie again, one hand trailing down his chest and heading for lower regions. Frankie's cock had gotten into the game as soon as Jim pushed him against the wall.

He edged closer to Jim, asking silently for more. Dropping a hand to Jim's ass, he dared to dig his fingers into the swell of muscle.

Jim grunted and yanked him nearer, roughly shoving his thigh between Frankie's legs. "You need something, huh?" he teased. "Come on, then. Rub against me. Just like that."

Frankie ground against his thigh, breathing noisily against Jim's neck. "Fuck, I'm gonna come. Jim, please," he pleaded, not sure what he wanted, only that he felt like he was hurtling forward, powerless to stop or turn around.

He barely registered it when Jim opened his pants enough to yank them down his thighs. But when Jim touched his cock, closing his fist around it, Frankie bit Jim's shoulder and thrust his hips once, twice, and then spurted, drenching Jim's hand with his come.

"Jesus," he whispered, "Jesus *Christ.*" His legs shook, and he leaned into Jim, comforted when Jim held him and didn't pull away.

"How was that for a first time?"

A giggle escaped Frankie. It was kind of like being drunk, a loose-limbed, floaty feeling. "You smug bastard. It wasn't my first time."

"Oh, what was it? A cow or a sheep? That's pretty much your only options back in Kansas, right?"

Frankie punched his arm. "Fuck off."

"Not yet." Jim grabbed his hand and guided it down until Frankie's fingers curved around the hard swell of his cock. "I have something for you to do first."

"Smug," Frankie reiterated, but he tugged at Jim's buttons and shoved down his shorts. Then Jim was in his hand. Although not being able to see each other had its drawbacks, he decided he liked exploring Jim's cock with just his fingers. It lay in his hand, thick and heavy, but somehow soft, too, and vulnerable. Jim's breathing grew more ragged when he rubbed his thumb over the wet head.

"Come on," Jim told him. "We can't take too long or—unh, fuck, just there, like that."

Frankie had to work to get the angle right, more used to a cock pointing the other way 'round, and then he stroked quickly, wondering if he was going to get hard again. If Jim kept making those soft moans, he wouldn't have any problem with it. He paused to lick his hand, getting it wet, easing the way. When Jim spilled over his fingers, he brought them up to his mouth, tasting. He'd never cared for the taste of his own come, but maybe—

"Ugh." He made a face and spat. "Sorry," he said quickly, worried Jim might get upset. "I've never liked the taste."

"Never enjoyed the finer things of life, then?" Jim didn't sound upset, just amused, and Frankie relaxed. He wanted to stay there, wanted Jim to hold him, but Jim was already pulling away, and yes, they couldn't linger or people would wonder. They had to get back to the barracks. So he tried his best to put his clothes to rights, willing the hectic flush from his face.

"See you—" Jim began, but Frankie grabbed his wrist and leaned down for another shy kiss.

"All right, then." Jim sounded fond. "Sleep well, Frankie."

"You too."

Jim squeezed his shoulder, and Frankie listened to the sounds of his footsteps dwindling away. He'd have to stare at Ed's empty seat in the ready room tomorrow. But he'd get to see Jim again too. It helped, knowing that.

He didn't sleep well. He woke in the middle of the night, sweaty, heart going a mile a minute from the nightmare that had seized him. It had been the pilot with the white parachute, the one George had killed, except *he* had been the pilot this time, hanging there in midair, listening to the purring engine of a 109 coming closer, unable to do anything except wait, knowing that any second, he would feel the bullets thudding into his body.

Curling around his pillow and drawing the blankets closer, he tried to forget it. Forgetting was impossible, though, and in the dark, with nothing to distract him, his mind kept circling back, replaying every second until at last he fell into a fitful, troubled sleep.

CHAPTER THIRTEEN

"THAT'S IT, darlin'," Jim murmured, bent over the engine, screwdriver and greasy rag in hand.

Frankie watched him for a few seconds, grinning as Jim kept cooing at the wiring.

"What do you want, Frankie?" Jim finally asked, squinting at him and tilting his cap up on his forehead.

"CO sent me out here to help clean wheel struts."

"And what got you that duty?"

He shrugged. "I got in a fight."

"A fight," Jim repeated.

"With Roy. Nothing serious." He rubbed his jaw. "Guy throws a wicked left." It hadn't been serious—it had been kind of stupid on Frankie's part, actually. He had been feeling so tense, like he had to let out some of his emotions or he'd go crazy. They hadn't flown a mission that day, the weather too cloudy, and Frankie had been shocked to discover he felt glad about it. He was relieved he wouldn't have to fly. That had never happened; he had always wanted to fly. Being in his plane made him happy, excited, eager, but all of those feelings had been absent, leaving only a steady undercurrent of relief. Panicked and angry, he had spent the day wandering restlessly around the base, trying to distract himself. When Roy had made some joke about Frankie not being the first of them to score a kill—"Not such a hotshot pilot now, is he?"— Frankie had growled that he'd show him how hot he was, and things had devolved from there.

Jim studied him for a few more seconds and then directed Frankie to the cleaning supplies and told him what to do. "I'll want those looking like new, Lieutenant."

Frankie threw him a mock salute. It was just them out there—the closest guys were at least thirty feet away and talking among themselves. So he said, "I heard you whispering sweet nothings to that engine."

"Feeling jealous, are we?"

Frankie stuck out his lower lip and sniffed loudly. "I didn't realize I was the other woman." He pretended to dab at his eyes.

Jim laughed and pulled off his cap. He settled it on Frankie's head, tugging it into place. "Enough malarkey, Lieutenant. I want those struts gleaming by dinner." Then he bent closer. "Think you could get a two-day pass for London next weekend?"

Frankie's heart sped up. "I think so."

"Do it. We'll get a hotel room." Jim's eyes centered on Frankie's mouth.

Swallowing, Frankie nodded. "Sounds swell." His voice cracked a little on the words, assaulted by a hundred ideas of what they could do with an entire weekend together.

Jim reached out and ran a gentle thumb over Frankie's jaw. "And don't get in any more fights between now and then. A split lip would be *very* inconvenient."

Getting a pass wasn't a problem. Surviving until the weekend began to seem more difficult with every day, however. They ran an escort mission on Tuesday and another on Wednesday, up at 0300 each time, counting down the anxious minutes until takeoff, then the long six to eight hours up in the air. On Tuesday they didn't encounter any fighters, but they did on Wednesday. Only a small group, though, and Frankie didn't see much action, now stuck being Tail-End Charlie. He got off a few shots and then his right gun jammed again. He experienced a few problems with the right engine, too, the oil temperature rising rapidly, then slowly falling back to a safer level. Jim spent all Wednesday night working on it, and he had it ready Thursday morning, though he was bleary eyed and unshaven as he helped Frankie into the cockpit. Frankie knew he looked just as bad. He kept having trouble sleeping, and his body ached with exhaustion.

They rendezvoused with the bombers over France. Below them the Army was crawling toward Paris, encountering stiff German resistance. It had been just over a month from the D-Day invasion, and they had made progress, but it wasn't coming quickly enough for Frankie's tastes. Why couldn't the bastards just give up? Today the target was a factory in eastern France. The bombers dropped their eggs despite heavy flak, but on the way out, they got bounced.

"Bogies, twelve o'clock high!"

A thick cloud of Me 109s and Fw 190s buzzed toward them. There had to be at least thirty of them. They closed rapidly, distant black blurs one second, and individual threats the next. Frankie's wing leader surged to the right, and he followed, keeping the turn tight. They zeroed in on a 109, and Lawson started firing, tracers bright little flares in the sky. The 109 flipped backward in a split-S, and Lawson dove too. Frankie tried to keep up, but had to jerk left to avoid a pair of 190s, one of which had smoke trailing from the wing. By the time he recovered, Lawson had disappeared. No point trying to find him in this mess, so he picked a likely target and went for it.

The Me 109 realized he was there a second before his bullets converged. Snap rolling, it corkscrewed out of danger. Frankie engaged the throttle and roared after it. Suddenly, the roiling fighters that had surrounded them disappeared, and they blazed forward into an empty sky. The 109 dropped down, but it was a lazy dive, taunting Frankie, daring him to follow. Frankie started to do just that, suffused with a grim pleasure at showing this overconfident Jerry that he had tangled with the wrong guy. And then some sixth sense pinged, danger prickling his skin.

He yanked the stick left so far he thought the rudder might snap off. Bullets sheared through the air where he had been, another Me 109 screaming past a second later, too close to follow him into the turn. But he had heard some of those bullets pinging against metal. He'd been hit, but he couldn't verify the extent of the damage. A quick scan of his instruments didn't show any immediate problems.

He circled back to the main force, only to find the fighting had tapered off, the Nazis disappearing into the clouds. Frankie located Lawson again and fell into position.

"Blue Two, this is Blue Three." That would be John Mason, number three in their flight. "You okay?"

"I got kind of chewed up, I think," Frankie replied, "but she seems to be flying okay. Why? Is the damage bad?"

After a pause that did nothing to reassure him, Mason finally said, "Not too bad."

"Let me know if you start having any problems," Lawson told him.

"Yes, sir." Frankie swallowed, wishing he could see more of his plane. He had been such an idiot to go chasing off after that 109 by himself. He could be dead right now. The realization, which hadn't had time to hit him during the heat of the battle, now made him break out into a cold sweat. His oxygen mask pressed against his mouth, digging into the skin hard enough to leave angry red lines behind, but he relished the discomfort at the moment, a tangible reminder he was still here, still breathing.

About fifteen minutes later, he noticed the precipitous drop on his fuel gauge.

Shit. Maybe a line had been punctured.

"Blue Leader," he said over the comm, "I'm losing fuel."

Lawson's voice crackled back to him. "Try to hold on. We'll be over friendly territory soon. Bail out if you need to."

"Yes, sir," Frankie replied, but a cold terror, different from the frenzied adrenaline of the fight, settled around his heart. He couldn't bail out. He'd be too vulnerable.

Part of him knew he was being irrational. There weren't any enemy aircraft around. No anti-aircraft guns. He'd be fine— probably safer than if he kept flying.

But he could see it in his mind. The white parachute. The pilot, defenseless. The quick rat-a-tat of the machine gun.

"Blue Two," Lawson said as they drew near the coast. "What's the situation?"

Not good. The fuel gauge was dipping dangerously low, and the left engine kept threatening to stall. "I'll make it," he said. "I know I can make it." He had to make it. He couldn't leave the cockpit; he just couldn't.

His left engine started to go half-way over the Channel. "Come on," Frankie breathed, feathering the controls, trying every trick he knew. Sweat drenched his shirt and cool runnels slipped down the side of his face.

"Bail out, Blue Two," Mason told him. "You're trailing smoke."

"No. I can make it," Frankie repeated. He didn't realize until later he had never even turned his radio on and no one could hear him. "I can make it."

The left engine stopped about a mile from base. He barely cleared the trees coming in, and he hit the runway hard, fighting with the stick to stay in control. Smoke billowed around him, and he could hear the blaring siren of a fire truck. The canopy stuck for a moment, but in a burst of adrenaline he shoved it open and tumbled out, stumbling onto the ground. He managed to get clear before the hoses started spraying foam. Medics pounced on him a minute later.

"I'm fine," he said, coughing to clear his throat. "I didn't get hit."

When he turned to look back at the Mustang, he had to put a steadying hand on the ambulance. The tail had been shredded, bullet holes formed a constellation across the fuselage, and the left engine was a charred mess.

"Frankie? Frankie!"

Jim came pelting toward him, breathing hard.

"I'm all right," Frankie told him, pushing up and standing straight.

Jim stared at him a second and then looked at the plane. "What the fuck is this?" he demanded.

"I tangled with an Me 109."

"No shit. And when it's this bad, you bail out. If that engine had gone out any sooner…." Jim scrubbed a hand through his hair, glaring. "What the hell were you *thinking*?"

"That you'd have my head if I didn't get your plane back to you," Frankie said, trying to make a joke of it.

But Jim took it like a punch to the gut. "Jesus. Are you serious?" His voice was bleak, shocked.

"No, of course that wasn't why. I just... I mean, I knew I could get back."

"It was one hell of a risk."

"I know. I'm sorry." Frankie gave him a placating smile. He couldn't admit to the fear that had kept him tethered to the cockpit. "Won't happen again."

"Better not." Jim suddenly slung an arm around his neck and dragged him down far enough to ruffle his hair. "I'll be pissed off if I have to go to London alone."

Squawking, Frankie wriggled free.

"Now go sit down before you fall down," Jim ordered. "God knows how long it's going to take me to fix this mess."

Leaving his aircrew to deal with the poor, battered Mustang, Frankie rode the ambulance to the hangars. Lawson chewed him out, too, and he had to suffer through the embarrassment of admitting he had chased off after that 109, practically gotten killed, and hadn't even scored a hit for his troubles.

When the debriefing finally ended, he dragged himself off to take a shower. He ran into George in their barracks.

"Jeepers, Frankie, you sure did a number on that plane!" George said as he collected clean clothes. "Can't believe you made it back here."

"Didn't feel like taking a bath in the Channel," Frankie replied and then headed for the showers, not in the mood to rehash the entire experience again.

The shower helped, and he finally stopped shaking as the lukewarm water sluiced the sweat from his body. After drying off, he went back to his bunk, the hut now thankfully empty, and collapsed on the mattress. He'd hardly closed his eyes before he was asleep.

He woke a few hours later. A low murmur of voices came from the other end of the hut, and he squinted at his watch. A little after seven. Damn, he'd missed supper. His mouth felt like it had been stuffed with cotton, and his head ached. His chest and neck were sore from slamming into the safety straps on the landing. Biting back a groan, he flopped onto his back, staring at the ceiling.

For a few blissful minutes, he was able to keep his mind blank. But then the memories welled up, little bubbles of fear and panic popping to the surface. Over all of it, like a slick patina of oil, floated his inability to bail out, even when it had almost killed him to stay in the plane.

How had this happened to him? He *loved* flying. He was good at it. He wasn't a coward. He'd chased that 109, hadn't he? Even if it had been stupid, it hadn't been the action of a coward. But right now... right now, he didn't know if he would be able to get back into that cockpit and fly again.

Finally he hauled himself upright and went to scrounge up some food. At least his appetite hadn't failed him. Then he went to find Jim. All he wanted was for Jim to put his arms around him, to have Jim's kisses drive away all his dark thoughts. That, of course, wasn't possible. Coming to a halt near his plane, Frankie watched wistfully as Jim and the rest of the crew crawled over the left wing, arguing about valves and engine parts. When Jim caught sight of him, he hopped down and came over.

"We'll be working on this all night, and I doubt we'll finish by tomorrow," Jim said. "Unless they find another plane for you, you'll be grounded." He scowled. "Anyway, even if they did find another plane, I wouldn't let you go up without checking it all over myself."

Frankie hated the wave of relief that swept over him. He wished he hadn't eaten supper after all, the food a heavy lump in his stomach as it churned with shame.

"How are you feeling?" Jim asked, perhaps catching something in his expression.

"Better," he made himself say. "I fell asleep, I was so blamed tired. Those dogfights take it out of a fella." He grinned. "But next time, I'll catch myself a Nazi." There. That had sounded all right, hadn't it? Confident and fearless. He glanced over at the plane and the rest of the crew. "Sure wish I could kiss you right now."

Jim smiled, sly and teasing. "I want to do a hell of a lot more to you than just kissing." He clapped Frankie on the shoulder. "Now go find someone else to bother. If I don't get your plane fixed up, I won't be able to go to London."

Frankie threw him a quick salute and started jogging in place. "Sir! Yes, sir!"

Laughing, Jim gave him a shove, and Frankie ran a few steps before settling into a walk.

CHAPTER FOURTEEN

JIM DID get the plane fixed, although they had to leave later on Saturday than they had planned. Frankie had spent Friday in a wretched state, torn between guilt and relief when the rest of the squadron got sent on a mission and he remained grounded. Sweating everyone out had been awful, the hours crawling by until finally the distant thrum of engines broke the silence. Then they had all rushed outside and counted off the incoming planes. Seven didn't return.

He and Jim took a series of trains to London and then walked from the station to a hotel recommended by a guy Jim knew. Seeing the bombed-out sections of London were enough to convince Frankie of the capriciousness of war. An entire house reduced to rubble while the house across the street still had geraniums in its window boxes. Whether you put it down to chance or luck, there was no reason there a person could grasp. Buzz bombs had been falling all summer, and by now, most Londoners simply went about their business even as the shriek of the rockets and air raid sirens filled the air. Rushing off to seek shelter was no guarantee of safety.

When they had gotten off the train at the station, Jim had asked him, "Dinner first or straight to the hotel?"

Frankie didn't think he could make it through dinner, not when Jim's left side had been pressed against him the entire train ride, warm and solid and promising. "Hotel," he said firmly, trying to ignore the flutter of nerves in his stomach. He wanted to be with Jim, but he was also afraid he would make a mess of it. If Jim wanted to fuck him… all he had were crude jokes to go on when it came to the mechanics of it.

The hotel had seen better days, but it wasn't too expensive, and the clerk didn't bat an eye when they only requested one room. Frankie ran his fingers up and down the jagged teeth of the key as they ascended a flight of stairs and then walked down the hallway to number fifteen. Jim slouched along at his side, hands in his pockets.

Frankie locked the door behind them again once they were in the room. Nothing fancy—just a bureau, a bed, a table, a lamp with a green shade, and an easy chair with a worn pillow. Blackout curtains had already been drawn, and Frankie moved cautiously to the bedside to flick on the lamp. He could feel Jim's eyes on the back of his neck.

Attempting to swallow down his nerves, Frankie reached into the pocket of his jacket before turning around. "I got something for you," he told Jim and held out a box of Mallo Cups. Jim had such a sweet tooth, and he still remembered stumbling on Jim eating the chocolate-covered coconut candies when they were back in California.

"Where did you get those?" Jim asked, grinning and immediately popping one into his mouth.

"My mother. I wrote asking her to try and find some. I knew she would, even with the rationing."

"Your mom sounds swell. Maybe I'll get to meet her someday."

"Sure." Frankie shoved his hands in his pockets to hide the fact they were twitching nervously. On the one hand, Jim wanting to meet his mother was a sign he thought this thing between them was going to last. On the other hand, well, he had never told his parents he was queer, and so Jim would have to be just a friend, and they'd have to be careful never to let their eyes or their hands linger too long on each other.

A small pool of light lapped across the floor, shining outward from the lamp. It stopped just at the edge of their shoes.

Jim kicked off his, wriggling his toes in his socks, and ripped open the yellow wrapper on another Mallo Cup. Then he shrugged out of his coat and tossed it on the easy chair. Frankie copied his movements, laying his own coat over Jim's. He fiddled with his collar, keeping his gaze on the floor, feeling more awkward by the second. But then Jim was there, his own hands replacing Frankie's. He popped the top button on Frankie's shirt. Then the next one. And the next. His gaze was steady, fixed on Frankie's face, and Frankie, after a quick look that took in Jim's soft mouth and the curve of his dark eyebrows, had to drop his eyes again. He looked down at his own white undershirt, watching as his nipples stiffened under the thin cotton, responding to Jim's touch. He blushed. Somehow, being with Jim was in a whole different ballpark from that night with Sergio in San Diego. He had been nervous then, too, but had been comforted by the knowledge that it was just the one night. If he made a total fool of himself, well, he wouldn't be seeing Sergio again. But he would be seeing Jim again, *wanted* to see him, always, and he desperately wanted this to be good, for Jim not to be disappointed.

Jim rubbed his thumb over Frankie's left nipple and then rested his palm against his chest. The tips of his fingers were a little cold where they brushed his collarbone, but the steady pressure felt like a pole propping him up. Like Frankie could collapse against it, but it would never let him fall.

"Your heart is beating so fast. Like a rabbit's," Jim murmured. His brown eyes were warm when he looked up, and he leaned in for a kiss.

Jim lingered over his lips, sometimes wandering to the corners of his mouth before returning. A taste of the sweet chocolate and coconut of the Mallo Cups remained on his tongue. Frankie's arms slipped around him, feeling the shift of muscles on his back under the khaki shirt.

"Come on," Jim said at last, tugging Frankie over toward the bed. Frankie sat on the edge of the blanket, flushed and a little dazed from the kissing.

Jim stood over him, his legs spread a little, and Frankie reached out and grabbed his belt, pulling at it.

"Impatient?" Jim asked, grinning and stepping closer.

He didn't bother answering, just undid Jim's belt and pressed his hand over Jim's crotch, cupping the bulge of his cock. The nerves had receded into the background, a restless shivering he could ignore as he lost himself in the sensation of Jim surrounding him, in the nuances of Jim's reactions, in all the things he had been too rushed to pay attention to the other times they had snatched a moment together.

Jim sucked in a breath at Frankie's touch and hastily stripped off his shirt. He pulled his undershirt over his head, too, leaving his torso bare. He'd seen Jim shirtless before, back in California, and on the rare, sunny day here, but it was different now. Now he was going to get to touch the jut of his collarbone and the dark hair on his chest. He'd lay his hand there and watch it rise and fall with Jim's breaths.

"You too," Jim said. "Come on, Frankie. You too."

So Frankie undressed, shedding clothes until he was down to his trousers, his bare toes curling against the scrap of thin carpet. He hesitated, but Jim was hopping around like a kid in a sack race, tugging his own pants off, so he pushed down his trousers, too, and kicked them away.

Jim crawled onto him a second later, pushing him farther onto the bed. They were both still wearing their shorts, and Jim still had on his socks. Frankie couldn't help pointing that out.

"My feet are cold," Jim groused. "We could have been posted to Italy. I bet it's warm there. Lovely sunshine. None of this blamed rain."

He settled his arms on either side of Frankie, his body almost on top of him, but shifted a little to the side, like he didn't want to overwhelm him with too much at once. His hair had been mussed when he pulled off his shirt, and the front part stuck up every which way.

Jim's skin felt hot where it pressed against his own—their arms, stomachs, part of their chests. Frankie's dick was getting wet and sticky in his shorts, and he scooted close enough to slide a leg between Jim's thighs. Jim took it as the invitation it was. He rolled his hips, rutting his cock against Frankie's leg with a groan. Frankie put his fingers in Jim's thick hair and dragged him into another kiss.

"Just let me look at you, just a second," Jim whispered, and Frankie reluctantly relinquished his mouth, letting Jim sit back on his knees. Frankie squirmed a little under his gaze. He'd put on weight since he'd enlisted, but he was still skinny. His cock was pushing out the cotton of his shorts.

Jim reached down and squeezed it.

"Shit," Frankie gasped, humping into the touch.

Jim let go and rubbed his hand on Frankie's stomach instead, scratching through the short, blond hairs curling up from his groin.

"Don't tease," Frankie protested. "Just—fuck, please, Jim."

A very smug grin this time, and then Jim popped the buttons on Frankie's shorts and slowly rolled them down. Frankie's cock bobbed free, and he tried not to make a desperate noise. Leaving his shorts tangled around his thighs, Jim slid down, stretching out on the bed, bringing his mouth level with Frankie's cock. Frankie held his breath, muscles taut with anticipation.

Jim lifted his cock, angling it toward his lips. He paused a moment, rubbing his thumb along the shaft, and Frankie let out his breath with a quaver. When Jim swirled his tongue on the head, licking up the fluid seeping out, Frankie had to grit his teeth to keep from crying out. "Oh, oh, *fuck.*"

That last escaped him, unable to stay silent when Jim took him into his mouth and sucked. He didn't go too deep at first, but he worked up to it, fluttering his tongue under the head, working spit down the shaft with his hand, finally sinking down, and Jesus, Frankie could feel the back of his throat, could press against it. He had to ball his hands into fists so he wouldn't just grab Jim's hair and push up as hard as he could.

He spared a brief thought to wonder if Jim was just naturally talented or if he had lots of practice with this, because he was going to come *right this minute* if Jim kept doing that with his tongue.

He tugged at Jim's hair. "I'm gonna—"

"Want you to," Jim mumbled, pulling off for a second, lips and chin glistening with spit. He jacked Frankie's cock with one hand and then took Frankie deep again, his other hand gripping his thigh.

Frankie couldn't stop the building wave of pleasure. His head rocked back, eyes squeezed shut, and his cry lodged fast in his throat, caught just in time. Jim swallowed the first pulse and then took his mouth away and switched to his hand, stroking him through the rest of it, getting his fingers wet with Frankie's come.

Chest heaving, Frankie squinted down to look at the mess on his stomach and Jim's hand. He'd lasted all of three minutes. Christ. Groaning, he rolled over, hiding his face in the pillow. "Sorry," he said, voice muffled.

Jim crawled back up his body and settled behind him, wrapping his arm around Frankie's stomach. He nuzzled the nape of his neck. "Don't apologize. You were gorgeous. So goddamn gorgeous."

Frankie found Jim's hand—the one not covered in come—and squeezed. Jim patted his ass and then wriggled around, stripping off his own shorts and wiping his hand clean before tossing them away. Frankie watched from his sprawl, appreciative at the sight of Jim's cock, stiff and flushed. He grunted as Jim pressed up against him again. Jim rolled his hips lazily, and his dick slid along Frankie's ass, heavy and blunt.

Frankie tried to get his bearings in the pleasant haze left from his orgasm. He managed to kick his shorts the rest of the way off, shoving them down to the end of the bed with his foot. Unbidden, he recalled all the lectures they'd had to sit through about VD and the dangers of clap, syphilis, and prostitutes. Bet the instructors had never thought about the boys themselves sleeping together. Frankie had to choke down a laugh at the insane absurdity of it all. Here he was thousands of miles from home, he'd almost died a few days ago, and the Army was worried about their morals, for Christ's sake—

"Hey, hey." Jim had noticed the sudden tension in his body. "You all right?"

"Yeah… just…." Frankie shook his head. "Just thinking."

"Well that won't do." Jim stroked a hand down his back. "Not when you've got me naked and hard right next to you."

God, he was being a crummy partner—leaving Jim hanging. "Sorry." He twisted around. "Sorry. I can… I mean…." He paused, putting one hand hesitantly on Jim's chest and tracing the sharp edge of his collarbone. "Did you want to fuck me?" he asked quietly, trying not to sound as uneasy at the prospect as he felt.

For once Jim didn't sling back a quick reply. His right hand was resting on Frankie's hip, and a socked foot kept brushing up and down Frankie's leg. "Some guys really like it," he said at last.

"Do you?"

A shrug.

"Oh." Frankie was taken aback. He had started to assume that Jim knew everything, had done everything. "I might not want to," he began slowly, "at least not this time." Jim wasn't long but he was thick, and Frankie couldn't quite imagine it fitting. Plus he was terrified he might be dirty there, and Jim would be repulsed. He had counted on Jim knowing how to go about these things. That Jim did not reminded him Jim only had four years on Frankie's eighteen. Sometimes he forgot that because Jim always seemed so sure of himself.

"I could suck you?" he tried again and was relieved when Jim grinned.

"Won't get any complaints from me."

First, though, Frankie had to pet his way down Jim's body, testing the softness of the sparse dark hair, discovering a ticklish spot on Jim's side, and ducking down to kiss his stomach with light, adoring pecks that had Jim laughing and pushing Frankie's head a little to the left where his cock curved upward.

Frankie pressed his nose in Jim's stomach and then turned his face to look at Jim's cock. He licked the tip and then ducked lower. Jim's sack was heavy in his hand and the scent of sweat and musk more powerful. Frankie tried to take Jim's balls in his mouth but was worried about his teeth grazing the sensitive skin and couldn't get the angle right. Still, what he did manage made Jim twist his fingers in Frankie's hair, urging him on.

It was probably so obvious he'd never done this before. Catching his breath, Frankie hitched himself up to try Jim's cock again, feeling determined. It filled up his mouth, pushing down his tongue.

He thought about that exam when he'd enlisted, his terror at the thought the doctor might know what he was when he hadn't gagged on that damn stick. Frankie found it ironic that now that he actually had a cock in his mouth, he did gag. He had to pull off, eyes watering.

"Easy," Jim murmured, rubbing the edge of Frankie's ear.

Frankie nodded, taking a deep breath, aware he was shaking a little from the intensity of it all.

He milked Jim's cock with his hand, watching the bead of fluid gather at the tip. He lapped it up and then sucked again, not trying to go as deep this time. There was no way to drown out the sounds they made—his muffled breaths, the wet pop of his lips, Jim's murmured encouragement. He tried moving his tongue a little more, remembering the way Jim had done it.

"That's so good." Jim sighed, his body relaxing a second and then tensing up. His orgasm caught both of them off guard, and Frankie choked and ended up catching most of the come on his face.

Wrinkling his nose, he tried to wipe it off and succeeded only in smearing it across his cheek.

"Christ, look at you," Jim said, sounding wrecked. He tugged Frankie up and actually started licking the semen off his face. And then they met each other's eyes and began laughing.

"I was awful," Frankie hiccupped.

"No." Jim grew more sober. "You were lovely. Don't think that." He gathered Frankie in, giving his ass a squeeze. "Wouldn't want anyone else."

"Yeah?" Frankie smiled, pleased.

Jim fished around in his trousers, lying nearby, and pulled out a handkerchief that he used to clean off Frankie's face.

They fell silent for a while, and Jim abandoned the handkerchief in favor of kisses, then just resting his forehead against Frankie's and holding him. Maybe he was thinking about having to watch Frankie's plane take off and vanish into the endless blue, never knowing if this time would be the last time. If, when the squadron returned, he would be met with a gap in the formation instead of the rumble of a Merlin engine taxiing toward him down the runway. Frankie was battling against his own fear, which seemed to have become a permanent part of him, like the white static in a radio transmission. He didn't want to fly another mission, and he didn't want to lose this connection to Jim, still so new and surprising. Those twin agonies battered his heart—having his joy of flying ripped away and the thought of dying when he had just found Jim.

Jim spoke first, and his words were lighthearted, hiding whatever solemn thoughts lurked behind the furrow between his brows that Frankie wanted to smooth away. "Next time I'm going to make you beg a little more. Payback for all the crazy stunts you pull out there in the old tin can."

"I might take that as an incentive," Frankie teased, trying to match his carefree tone. "I'll make it two 109s next time instead of just one."

Jim gripped his shoulders. "Don't you dare."

And yes, maybe it was too much to joke about such a thing now, when they were tangled together, Jim probably still able to taste him on his tongue.

After a few more minutes, Jim extricated himself from Frankie's sated limbs. He flipped out the light and stumbled over to the window to lift the curtain and crank open the window, letting in a slight breeze. On his way back to bed, he reached out to grab a pack of cigarettes from his coat. He settled back against the headboard, pulling Frankie up so Frankie was resting on his chest, and lit a cigarette.

It had gotten dark, a darkness that belied the sounds of traffic in the street below. "I wish I could see London all lit up," Frankie murmured, rubbing his nose against Jim's collarbone. "My parents still don't have electricity up at the ranch. I'll never forget that view of New York when we pulled out of the harbor."

He grabbed for the cigarette and Jim gave it to him, hitching his arm a little tighter around Frankie.

"One of my cousins lived on a farm outside of LA for a while. We went out there sometimes, and I remember how dark and quiet it was." Jim smiled. "I liked that part okay, but I missed having a soda fountain in walking distance. And the cows smelled pretty bad."

Frankie snorted. "City boy."

"Guess so." Jim reclaimed his cigarette, taking a drag before stubbing it out in the ashtray. "You going back to Idaho after all this is over?"

"Oh, so now you believe I'm from Idaho, huh? All it took was me putting out to convince you?"

He could feel the thrum against his cheek as Jim's laugh vibrated in his chest. "Might still call you Dorothy, though. You haven't shaken that farm boy innocence yet."

Frankie twisted his neck to look up at him. "You plan on doing something about that?"

Jim smirked in reply and bent down for a kiss, messy and slow.

"I don't want to go back to Idaho," Frankie admitted when Jim released him. He smoothed a hand over Jim's chest, resting his thumb under one of his nipples. "But I... I don't know what I'll do." Before these last, hellish weeks, he would have said he wanted to keep flying. But now.... He blinked hard to keep back the tears.

"Hey. You okay?"

"Yes." He didn't want to talk about it or think about it. So he flicked his tongue over Jim's nipple, guessing it would be a surefire way to distract him. Jim hummed, low in his throat, and stretched, hand coming up to cup Frankie's head and keep him in place. Frankie obligingly kept licking and even sucked a little, his right hand drifting lower to find out if other parts of Jim were equally eager to pick up where they had left off.

FRANKIE WOULD have been fine with staying in all night, curled up in the bed, but Jim said they needed dinner and he wanted a drink.

Down in the lobby, Jim pulled a bellboy aside and asked him if he had any clubs to recommend.

"The Arts and Battledress Club is always a favorite of the lads, but...." He paused, looking between Frankie and Jim. "I think you gents would prefer The Crown and Two Chairmen on Dean Street. More your kind of crowd."

Frankie tugged at his collar, hot and embarrassed. Was everybody going to be able to *tell,* just by looking at them? Jim slung an arm around his shoulders and steered him outside. "We can relax a little here, yeah?" he said. "No MPs looking over our shoulder. No brass waiting to chuck us out."

Frankie nodded, trying to loosen the tight knots in his shoulders.

They took a cab, careening through the darkened streets, its headlights turned off and the parking lights dimmed by two sheets of newsprint. They had just stopped by the curb in front of the club when the air raid sirens started up and the whine of a buzz bomb filled the air. A few people started rushing off to the nearest shelter, but most people kept on walking or talking. Frankie flinched at the noises. They heard the echoing boom when the bomb hit, but he couldn't tell where it had landed. Jim heaved a breath and leaned down to pay the cabby. Then he tugged Frankie into the club.

Dim lights and a wall of hazy cigarette smoke greeted them. A saxophone and trumpet ran up and down a scale, and then a woman's voice joined them, singing softly. Quite a few people were dancing, and Frankie's stomach jumped a little when he realized that some of the couples were men, as well as one with a woman dressed mannishly who twirled a blond girl in her arms.

Frankie narrowed his eyes at the speculative look on Jim's face. "I am not dancing with you," he declared.

"I'd let you lead," Jim coaxed.

"No. I'm a disaster—two left feet."

Jim shrugged, although he seemed a little disappointed, and led the way over to a booth near the back wall. He didn't sit across from Frankie but slid into the seat next to him, draping his arm behind Frankie's shoulders. They ordered some supper, and Jim insisted on a bottle of champagne.

"What are we celebrating?" Frankie asked.

"The fact that I ended up making love to you instead of throttling you," Jim retorted.

129

"Making love." Frankie laughed, even as something warm kindled in his chest at Jim's choice of words. "I'm not Rita Hayworth, you know."

Jim turned his head so he could run his eyes up and down Frankie's body. "Maybe not, but I wouldn't mind you in a pair of stockings and a little strapless number."

Frankie gaped. "You—what?" he stuttered. "Really?"

Jim eyed him over the rim of his champagne flute. "That a problem?"

"I don't know." Frankie squirmed a little. "I never thought about doing that."

"Relax." Jim rubbed his thumb over Frankie's neck. "It's not really my thing. But when you mentioned Rita Hayworth, I just thought of it."

"Oh."

Jim kept on rubbing circles into his skin. "If I can't even get you to dance with me, I doubt I'd have much luck in that department."

"I would dance with you!" Frankie protested. "But I meant it when I said I was terrible."

"Maybe some time when we're alone, then."

"No, we could. Off in a dark corner."

Jim smiled. "A bit later."

Frankie drank some more champagne, relaxing against Jim's arm. It felt so strange to be doing this in public. His eyes strayed to the dance floor again, fixing on a man with the same olive skin as Sergio. He moved smoothly, mouth stretching in a smile.

"Hey." Jim gave him a shake. "Don't pay attention to them. I didn't bring you here to ogle other men."

Frankie grinned. "Jealous?" Although Jim actually did look upset, mouth pressed into a thin line.

"Sorry," Frankie murmured. "Maybe you should kiss me."

Jim did—slowly and thoroughly. Frankie was out of breath when he sat back. Out of breath and very aroused. He put his hand on Jim's thigh, fingers pressing along the seam of his trousers.

"Ah, fuck." Jim caught his hand, drawing it away. "First we eat. Then we're going back to the hotel."

"What happened to dancing?"

"Forget dancing," Jim said and kissed him again.

When they did stumble back to their room, Frankie taking three tries to get the key in the lock, he felt drunker than he actually was, head whirling dizzily. As soon as the door shut behind them, he shoved Jim up against the wall, holding him still while he kissed him and then sucked his way down his neck. Jim groaned, his fingers digging into Frankie's shoulders. Frankie decided he liked being taller than Jim. Liked it very much because he could cover Jim with his body, enclosing him, making sure he paid attention to nothing but this, nothing but Frankie's mouth on him. By the way Jim was panting and fumbling with his belt, he liked it too.

Frankie sank down to his knees, yanking at Jim's trousers.

"Wait, wait," Jim begged, "I have to see this, have to see you." He flipped on the overhead light, and Frankie squeezed his eyes shut against the sudden brilliance.

"Sorry." Jim's fingers petted through his hair. "But I just had to watch. Pictured you like this so many times...." His voice trailed off into a ragged breath.

Frankie nuzzled his thigh, smiling up at him. He ran his hands over Jim's legs, the dark hairs tickling his palms, and around to squeeze his ass before focusing on his goal. Jim had gotten hard quickly, and his cock was right in front of Frankie's mouth, which watered at the memory of that thick length filling him. He licked his lips and then sucked in the tip, sinking down the shaft. Jim gave a wordless cry, and his hips bucked, his fingers tightening in Frankie's hair to hold him still while he fucked into his mouth.

Frankie breathed in through his nose, chin getting wet with spit, determined not to gag. He rubbed his thumbs over Jim's hipbones, pressing closer, trying to show him that this was fine, that he loved this, loved Jim using his mouth.

"Oh Christ." After a few minutes, Jim started to sound wrecked and his hips flexed faster. Frankie kept sucking, even

131

though his jaw had begun to ache. "You're so beautiful. Just… just…." He pushed deep, fingers buried in Frankie's hair. Warm spurts filled Frankie's mouth as he came, and this time, Frankie swallowed some before resorting to his handkerchief. Coughing, he collapsed against Jim's knees, lips covered in spit and come, so hard it was almost painful.

"Jim," he muttered, hoarse and desperate. "Please."

"Anything, baby, anything." Jim slid down, arms coming around him, kissing Frankie's forehead. He eased his buttons apart, and Frankie drew in a shaky, relieved breath. One, two strokes, and he came in Jim's hand, abdomen clenching, biting his lip but unable to stop a high, wordless moan from escaping.

They stayed there on the floor, Frankie resting his head on Jim's shoulder, Jim rubbing his back and peppering his hair and ears with kisses. When they finally roused and made it the few feet to the bed, leaving their clothes in a messy heap, Frankie gravitated into Jim's arms again. He had to scoot down until his feet dangled off the end of the mattress to be able to lay his head on Jim's chest, but he didn't mind. Jim had still possessed the presence of mind to turn off the light, and it only took a few minutes before Frankie fell asleep.

ON SUNDAY morning he woke up slowly, relishing being able to laze in bed instead of leaping to his feet. They had shifted during the night, and now he was curled against Jim's back. For a few seconds he just held still, breathing Jim's scent. Then he leaned forward and kissed Jim's shoulder, slipping an arm around his waist. Jim carried more fat and muscle on his frame than Frankie did, and his stomach was a little rounder. He wasn't overweight, but there were some lovely soft spots that Frankie could stroke. His fingers found the trail of hair leading down to Jim's groin, and he followed it. Jim's cock wasn't even half-hard yet, and he gathered it in his palm, just holding it for a few moments and then petting lightly. Jim groaned.

"Having fun?" Jim asked, voice scratchy from sleep.

"Mmmhmm." Frankie huddled closer, kissing Jim's neck and licking at his earlobe. His own cock was filling rapidly, and it poked against the top of Jim's ass, sensitive and eager.

Jim started rocking into Frankie's hand, breath speeding up. "Stick it in between my thighs," he said.

Now that was a fantastic idea. Frankie licked his hand first, getting his cock wet, smearing some of it on Jim's thighs. His cock fit snugly against Jim's balls, and Frankie started thrusting. His hand attending to Jim lost momentum as all his attention centered on the friction and heat. He mouthed at the back of Jim's neck, squeezing his eyes shut and soaking in Jim's smell and the weight of his body, pressed so closely to Frankie. Last night had been a big rush, fantastic, but over quickly. This was slower. He'd never experienced anything as intimate and sweet as being wrapped around Jim, every one of Jim's groans and hitched breaths transferred to him where they twined together.

When he came, the sound he made was more of a sob than anything else. He lay there shaking, trying to get his breath back. Jim got a bit impatient and took Frankie's hand in his own, moving it up and down his cock.

"Wait," Frankie managed to say, and Jim stopped, although he twitched irritably.

"What is it?" His voice was strained. "Dammit, Frankie, I'm about to—"

Frankie struggled to untangle them, his come smearing all over Jim's thighs. He pushed Jim onto his back and knelt between his legs, then scooted down. Taking a deep breath, he lowered his mouth toward Jim's cock.

Jim heaved a deep breath, his fingers brushing through Frankie's hair and then gripping harder. Frankie kept his eyes tilted up to Jim's face as he slid his lips around the head of his cock. Jim's muscles tensed, and his head thumped back onto the pillow. He didn't last long, gritting out, "Frankie, I'm gonna come," soon enough that Frankie could pull off and milk Jim through it.

"You like that," Jim said to him when they were once again settled under the blankets and Frankie had cleaned them up a bit

133

with a washcloth. "Can't get enough of my cock in your mouth. Every time, you wanted it."

"Yep," Frankie said, not even blushing, because it was true. "Well, I like it up to the part where you come," he amended. "The taste...." He stuck out his tongue.

Jim laughed. "Afraid I can't help that part."

"Just so long as you don't mind. You've probably been with guys who are a lot better than I am."

"I don't mind." Jim shook his head, smiling. "You're such a doll," he murmured, hand warm on Frankie's chest, his eyes roaming over Frankie's face. "Can't believe you ended up in my plane."

"Our plane," Frankie corrected.

Jim chuckled. "Our plane," he agreed. His eyes narrowed as Frankie went a little tense in his arms, his easy smile fading. "What?"

Frankie shrugged. It had been all right for a second, but then thinking about the plane had made him think about being trapped in it, so goddamned afraid of bailing out.

"Frankie?" Jim coaxed.

He shouldn't talk about it with Jim. Jim couldn't find out what a coward he was. But it clawed in his throat, demanding to be voiced. "I didn't think it would be like this," he admitted after a moment, voice hardly above a whisper. "I knew I'd be scared. I wasn't *that* stupid. But it was supposed to be dogfights—fast and kind of thrilling. And instead...." He trailed off, unable to put into words the terror of seeing that pilot sliced into ribbons by bullets, of the oppressive silence of the sky during a long mission, of the almost graceful curve of a bomber plummeting toward the ground. And most of all that frozen sensation that had kept him pinned in the cockpit, even as his plane fell apart around him. Ducking his head, he looked away so Jim couldn't see the moisture gathering in his eyes.

Jim moved closer, putting his arms around him and tucking his head against his shoulder. "We'll get through it," he said. "It'll be all right."

Frankie wasn't sure he believed him, but was grateful all the same.

"SO TELL me more about yourself," Frankie said as they leaned on the railings of a bridge, watching the water swirl by far beneath them. They had finally dragged themselves out of bed, scrounged up some breakfast, and were now wandering around London. It was nice not to have a particular destination in mind, to have a break from military punctuality. Not that Roy, for one, had ever quite grasped that concept.

"What do you want to know?" Jim asked, lighting a cigarette. He hadn't shaved, and he looked a bit scruffy and unkempt. Frankie, who couldn't have grown a decent beard if his life depended on it, resisted the urge to rub his knuckles over Jim's jaw. "I already told you about my brother and my parents."

"And your uncle and the auto repair shop, yeah. And I know you have a sweet tooth, are obsessed with spark plugs, and can be a real asshole sometimes. But beyond that...."

Jim smoked meditatively for a moment. "I want a leather jacket," he said at last. "I've wanted one since I was eleven and saw a guy wearing one in a bar. Not a cheap one, either, but something real nice, the leather soft as butter."

Frankie took a moment to appreciate the image of Jim in a leather jacket. "I'll buy you one when we go home. I'll buy you a leather jacket, and you can buy me a motorcycle."

"Hang on now," Jim protested. "One of those is a hell of a lot more than the other."

Frankie pouted. "But I'm worth it, ain't I, baby?"

Jim snorted. "You have a high opinion of yourself, don't you?" He nudged Frankie's shoulder with his own. "But yeah, I guess you're worth it."

Grinning, Frankie looked back out over the river. "Where have you always wanted to travel to?"

"Jeez, Frankie, I don't know. Hawaii?"

"We'll go there, then. To some beach, even though I get sunburned no matter how much lotion I slather on. I always wanted to drink one of those cocktails—with the little umbrella and the fruit, you know?"

Jim didn't say anything, and Frankie finally turned to look at him. "What?" he asked, puzzled by the look on Jim's face.

"You're talking about a lot of 'after,'" Jim said. "Are you... serious?"

Was he serious about wanting to stay with Jim after the war? He hadn't really thought about it—had just thought about the sex, frankly, at first. But now he'd had that, and—well, he did want more. He liked Jim. Liked him very much. Maybe even—

"Yes." He sounded breathless. "Is that okay?"

Jim's eyes softened, and he nodded. "I'd like that."

"Good." Frankie leaned closer, dropping a quick kiss onto Jim's hair.

CHAPTER FIFTEEN

THEY PUT off going back to base as long as possible, but finally caught a late train, hitched a ride in a lorry, and arrived back bleary-eyed and exhausted on Monday, very early in the morning. It was still dark, and Jim simply clapped him on the shoulder before stumbling off to his bunk. Frankie crawled into his own bed and caught about forty minutes of sleep before they were awoken for a mission.

But the mission didn't happen, thanks to a heavy cloud bank rolling in. Foggy Belmont thought it might clear, though, and so they had to remain on call, shuffling around the ready room. A few guys organized a football game, but Frankie was too tired to participate. He couldn't fall back to sleep, though, because there was a chance they would still go up, and his stomach kept clenching at the thought.

He wandered over to where Jim was working on the Mustang, but Jim, greasy and irritable, shooed him away, saying that he couldn't have "idiot pilots" hanging about during delicate operations. Maybe Jim's bad mood had something to do with the fact that they couldn't touch or kiss. Frankie sure felt bummed. And now that Ed was gone, he didn't have anyone to talk to about it. No one to share the kind of giddy feeling that had been welling up whenever he thought of their conversation on the bridge.

That night, without Jim sleeping next to him, there was nothing to take his mind off the bad dreams, either. He was hanging in the air, looking over a beautiful green field, parachute drifting on a gentle breeze. But he knew the bullets were about to slice into him. He couldn't do anything to stop it. He jolted awake, a scream gurgling in his throat.

Shaking, he pressed his face into the pillow, the thin linen gradually soaking through with tears he couldn't seem to stop.

"DAMN, FRANKIE, you look like shit," Roy told him the next day as they huddled in the briefing room at 0500 hours. "Didn't you just have the weekend off?"

"Maybe he needs a visit to the Flak Home," George said, plopping down next to them. While Frankie had been gone, they'd flown another mission, and George had added another Me 109 to his kill list.

"I'm fine," Frankie snapped. "I want to go shoot something."

"Atta boy." George clapped him on the shoulder.

That day, the briefing officer informed them, they would be going on a strafing mission instead of escorting bombers. As the Army drew closer to Paris, the Air Forces were targeting anything that might soften up the Germans' resistance, such as trains, trucks, radio relays, and airfields.

He'd hardly slept at all, but he felt angry rather than exhausted—angry at himself for being a damn coward, angry at the goddamned Nazis for starting this war, angry they'd lost Ed, angry that every mission he had to fly increased the odds that he'd get killed and wouldn't come back to Jim. He held on to that anger, trying to burn away the fear that wanted to overtake it as he strapped on his parachute.

He mustered a small smile for Jim but couldn't keep it up long. Jim took in his tired eyes and managed to squeeze Frankie's hand as he got him settled in the cockpit. "You okay?" he asked quietly so Henry wouldn't hear.

"Yes," he snapped, sick of people asking him that question. "I'm going to blow up an airfield. Or something."

Jim was unfazed by the tension vibrating in his voice. "Watch yourself, all right? We just repainted the nose."

Frankie rolled his eyes, knowing now that Jim hid his concern for Frankie behind his concern for the plane.

"Get off," he said, waving a hand. "I'll see you in a few hours."

If it had been another day—hell, another universe where there was no war—Frankie would have enjoyed the flying they had to do. Strafing missions required you to fly close to the ground, and you had to be alert every second, paying attention to obstacles, often using brute force to fight the drag on the stick, constantly adjusting speed and position. But he was so tired, and it dulled his reactions, adding to the looming panic in the back of his mind.

He tried to stoke his anger, following George, who was a wing leader on this mission, into a series of tight curves as they paralleled a river winding along below them.

They did eventually stumble on an airfield. It popped up over the next tree line. The Nazis had tried to camouflage some of the planes, but you couldn't hide it really, especially not from this close.

"I'll head left, you head right," George said over the radio, and Frankie peeled off, already aiming his machine guns at a Messerschmitt, a sitting duck there on the ground. The bullets pinged off the concrete and then hit the plane, chewing into it. The explosion slammed him into his straps, and he pulled up, heart pounding, and aimed his sights at another.

He didn't see the two men ducking out from under the plane and sprinting toward cover until he had already fired. One of them went down, falling into a limp huddle. The Mustang hurtled past. His sights zeroed in on an Fw 190 that had a crumpled propeller, and he kept firing. Then his damned guns jammed.

He wished they had jammed ten seconds ago. If they had, that nameless German Frankie had just killed in nothing like a fair fight might still be alive.

"I'm picking up some machine gun fire," George said. "Let's get out of here."

They started running low on fuel before they found any other likely targets, so the flight turned back to home. Frankie flew mechanically, most of his mind grappling with his thoughts, trying to force them into order. He wanted to deny the wish about his guns.

After all, he was supposed to kill the enemy. And that man had been the enemy. He'd been a member of the German Army.

But he must have been so frightened in those seconds before his death, with the Mustang screaming toward him.

This was why he had chosen the Air Forces, for God's sake. Because he didn't want to be down in the mud blasting a machine gun. Against another fighter pilot, it was a match of speed and skill. The other man had a *chance*, and you could be proud of a victory.

Gritting his teeth, Frankie slammed a hand into the instrument panel, feeling the shock even through his thick glove. It didn't matter. It didn't *matter*. He wasn't going to let this get to him.

"PAINT LOOKS okay," Jim commented when Frankie slid out of the cockpit.

But Frankie couldn't handle their usual banter, not now. "The guns jammed," he snarled. "Thankfully I didn't have an Me 109 on my tail. Maybe you should spend less time nagging me and more time doing your job." It was completely unfair, of course. The mechanics did their best, but they couldn't prevent every problem, not in combat situations.

But Jim just said, "We'll fix it."

And that made Frankie more upset because he wanted Jim to be angry, to yell at him so he wouldn't feel so badly about yelling back.

Appalled, he realized he was about to start crying, and he turned away, walking and then breaking into a run, ignoring Jim calling after him. He ran into the nearest toilet and splashed some water on his face, stomach roiling with nausea.

"Frankie." It was Jim, knocking on the side of the wall, carefully avoiding looking at him. "Can I come in?"

He wanted to ignore Jim, but he had to get to the debriefing anyway. George was probably looking for him.

"Hey," Jim said when Frankie gestured for him to step inside.

140

Frankie met his dark brown eyes, warm with concern, for a moment, and then looked at his feet. "It was just a rough mission. I'm sorry I yelled at you."

Jim nodded. "You look like you could use this." He reached into his pocket and pulled out one of the candy bars he always had squirreled away, then held it out.

Frankie took it gratefully, tore back the paper and bit into the sweet chocolate. It settled his stomach a little.

Jim glanced around and then herded Frankie farther inside, into one of the shower stalls, partially shielded from the rest of the room. He crowded close, reaching up to tilt Frankie's head down so he could kiss him.

"I've been wanting to do that since we got back from London," he confessed.

"You're just regretting giving me the candy," Frankie said, finding he could still smile after all. "Wanted a taste of it."

Jim wrinkled his nose. "That's somewhat disgusting. And not true."

He could still laugh too.

"What happened?" Jim asked softly. "You don't have to tell me, but maybe, I don't know, maybe it would help."

Frankie shook his head, scrubbing a hand over his nose and sniffing.

"All right." Jim gave him another kiss. "Come meet me after dinner. We'll play poker or something."

"Okay." Frankie cleared his throat. "Thanks. I'm fine. It was just... well, I have to get to the debrief."

"Yep." Jim stood aside. "And I'll get to work on that jammed gun. Maybe I'll try putting in a whole new one."

After dinner he did go find Jim, and they settled into a corner of Jim's barracks. Jim shuffled the cards, and Frankie poured a handful of pennies onto the table to use for betting.

"My mother would say you're corrupting me," Frankie commented, taking the cigarette Jim handed him. "Smoking, drinking, cards," he lowered his voice a little, "sex."

"That is a pretty damning list." Jim laid down two cards and picked up new ones. "Although it seems to me, you've been a willing participant."

"Guess I have." Frankie looked up from his cards to give Jim a smile. "Besides, I'd never tell my ma about all this. She'll love you when she gets to meet you." He faltered. "I mean, if you ever wanted to come visit."

Jim leaned back in his chair, sighing. "Traveling to Kansas, huh? The things we do for love."

That was the second time Jim had referred to his feelings for Frankie as love. Always in a lighthearted way, of course, that might not be serious, but still, it lifted his heart. But if Jim knew how he could hardly make himself climb into that plane anymore, if he knew how deeply the deaths of those Germans had affected him—he didn't know if Jim would love him then. Jim nudged his foot. "Are you folding or what?"

"I'll fold." Frankie laid his cards down. It had been a bum hand.

Jim swept the little pile of pennies into his palm and then shuffled and dealt. "Speaking of corrupting you," he said in a low voice, "the next time we're alone, I think I'd like you to fuck me."

That made him sit up. He stared at Jim. "Really?" he stammered and then blushed.

Jim smirked. "Yep. Don't think I haven't seen the way you stare at my ass when I'm bent over the engine."

"Jeepers, don't talk about it here," Frankie hissed, grabbing his jacket and folding it over his lap.

"Awww, poor baby, you getting hard?"

Frankie glared.

"What do you say, though?" Jim asked, and he sounded almost hesitant, a little unsure. "That something you would like?"

"Are you kidding? I'd love that. Just thinking about it...." He took a deep breath. "I can't promise it would be great, the first time," he continued, scratching his neck. "I mean, well, it might take a while to figure out." Not to mention he'd probably only last five seconds once he slid inside Jim.

"Don't worry. We'll practice lots," Jim assured him, smiling.

He groaned. "Torture a guy, why don't you?"

They played until Jim had won all the pennies, and then Frankie said good night and went back to his own barracks. He was sure they would be up at 0300, as usual. God, what he wouldn't give for a week of uninterrupted sleep.

CHAPTER SIXTEEN

ANOTHER WEEK of escort missions and strafing runs dragged by. Frankie kept having the same dream, where he was stuck in the parachute, waiting for the bullets to hit him. This morning the squadron got rousted out of bed at 0400—an extra hour of sleep, like fucking Christmas came early, as Roy put it. They were scheduled for another strafing run in the vicinity of Le Mans. Frankie drank three cups of coffee, not caring if he had to struggle with the relief tube that was the only option for dealing with a full bladder while in flight. The tube in George's plane had gotten frozen the other day, and he'd ended up with a lapful of his own piss when he tried to use it. *That* had been a colorful bout of swearing they'd all been treated to upon landing. But he'd take the possibility for humiliation over falling asleep in midair. He'd slept, but it had been a restless sleep, and it seemed like he'd woken up every hour. The dream had come just before the orderly came to wake them, and Frankie had grabbed the poor man's arm, clawing at his shirt for a breathless second until awareness returned to him.

After the briefing, he signed for his survival kit and gathered the rest of his gear, then joined the controlled madness of preflight checkups and refueling as he jogged toward his plane. Jim, Henry, and the rest of his crew were there, still wearing jackets to ward off the chill of early morning. Frankie jammed on his helmet, took another step toward the plane, and froze.

It was a strange sensation, his conscious brain telling his body to keep moving, to *get into the plane, goddammit*, while his subconscious rebelled, drowning in the deepening reservoir of panic and fear that had been filling steadily over the past weeks.

"Frankie?" It was Jim, wiping his hands on a rag. "You're all set."

He didn't respond, worried that if he opened his mouth the only thing that would come out would be "I can't."

But he could. He could do this. He wasn't going to fall apart in front of his entire squadron, in front of Jim.

"Frankie?" Jim was looking worried, hand moving to touch Frankie's arm, and God, that would be the worst, he really would break down if Jim's concern became tangible, a haven into which he wanted to disappear and never reemerge.

Somehow he lurched back into motion, fingers clumsily buckling the strap of his helmet. As always, Jim followed him up to the cockpit to help him get situated, the flight suit and various survival gear an awkward weight. Frankie was already sweating, his mouth dry from—from whatever that had just been.

"Thanks," he managed to say to Jim, and Jim nodded, although the concern hadn't vanished from his eyes.

He didn't say anything, though, just gave Frankie's helmet its usual rap with his knuckles. When he jumped down, the panic surged again, but Frankie fought it off, finding refuge in the routine of checking the mags and getting cleared for takeoff. He taxied onto the runway, joining the conveyor belt of P-51s lining up, noses all pointed at the sky.

The humming monotony of the flight over the Channel brought a measure of calm. But he couldn't help wondering if he was going to get like this before every mission and, if so, how many more times he would be able to force himself into the cockpit.

He felt so... ashamed at his reaction. Never had he imagined it would affect him like this, not when he had loved flying so much, not when he was *good* at flying. But he didn't love it anymore, and maybe he was good at it, but it no longer filled him with pride. He couldn't be proud of shooting down defenseless men. Dogfights were one thing. Helping to drop bombs, to mow down men running from you on the ground... it made him sick. That, perhaps, was an emotion he did not need to feel shame for, but when it came down to it, he was afraid, afraid of his own death. He remembered telling Pete the only thing he feared was losing a limb, and a bitter laugh jolted out of him at how naïve he had been, to imagine death wouldn't scare him. It did. Oh God, it did.

He was a coward, and if Jim knew…. That scared him almost as much, the idea of losing Jim's love and affection. Every time he went up into the air, the odds increased that he would die, but if he didn't, he might lose Jim anyway, his love turning to scorn at the proof of Frankie's cowardice.

By the time they neared Le Mans, he had managed to reduce the panic to a dull throbbing. He had been assigned as George's wingman again, and when he spotted a train about a half a mile to the north, he radioed him the position. They drew closer, and Frankie aimed his guns at the long string of boxcars. No way to tell what was inside, but it didn't matter. Even if the train was empty, its destruction would mean one less war equipment transport. But as they approached, the sides of one of the boxcars fell away, revealing an anti-aircraft gun hidden inside. It started firing, tracking their path. Frankie pushed the throttle hard, and the Mustang accelerated, thundering ahead. He kept up his fire on the train, George doing the same behind him.

The car in front of him blew up. Shrapnel filled the air—bits of metal and wood exploding into hundreds of pieces. He pulled up as hard as he could and popped free of the deadly cloud a second later. He looked back to see George fly past where he had just been, guns blazing. Another car blew, this time expanding into a huge fireball. George flew right into it.

"George!" Frankie screamed over the radio. "George, are you okay?"

He turned around, flying back to the train and its shattered wreckage. The anti-aircraft gun had stopped. Why, he wasn't sure. Maybe George had hit it. Dipping lower, he scanned the ground. The charred remains of George's plane lay in the ditch alongside the tracks. Fire still licked along the fuselage, devouring the wings.

Frankie craned his neck, searching for signs of a parachute, but he knew it was pointless. There had been no time to escape. Heart heavy, he finally flew away to rejoin the squadron.

THE WORST part was telling Roy. He took the news quietly as they stood outside the briefing room back on base.

"I... it happened so quickly," Frankie said uselessly, helmet dangling from his fingers.

Roy stared down at the ground for a long minute. "Only a matter of time before another of us bought the farm," he finally muttered and walked away.

Later, though, Frankie found him sitting in the pilot's lounge, smoking and looking at a little pile of photos that must have belonged to George.

"Do you mind?" Frankie asked, hovering by the chair next to him, and Roy shook his head, gesturing for Frankie to sit.

"I'll have to send these back to his mother," Roy commented, flipping through the pictures. He paused and then asked, "Do you think maybe he could have been hit by the guns before the boxcar blew up?"

"Maybe." Frankie knew why Roy would want that to be the case. Believing that George had been killed by a bullet was a hell of a lot more bearable than imagining him being burned alive.

Roy nodded. "I think that's what I'll write regardless."

"Probably best."

They sat silently for a while, Roy studying each photo, over and over. He stopped at one of himself and George, perched on the wing of George's Mustang and laughing. Roy ran his thumb over the edge. "You know, I never understood Ed," Roy said slowly. His eyes flickered to Frankie. "Or you. How you could... be like that."

Frankie's hands curled into unconscious fists, his gut suddenly tight with panic. Roy had never said anything, or George for that matter, but he had been stupid to think they hadn't realized he was queer. Roy might blame him for what happened to George—report him to the CO.

"I didn't understand," Roy repeated. "But now, I think I sorta do." He thumbed the photo one last time and then shoved it back in with the others, stuffing them into an envelope.

After Roy left, Frankie downed the rest of his coffee and went to find Jim. He was out at the plane, of course, hard at work despite the late hour. Frankie leaned against the fuselage, watching him for a few minutes. They exchanged brief smiles, but the presence of the other crew members kept him from touching Jim the way he wanted. As it had so many times, his memory drifted back to that wonderful weekend in London. The taste of Jim's skin against his tongue, how his muscles flexed under his fingers, the sounds he made—all sprang vividly into his mind.

"Want a smoke?" Frankie asked him, jerking his head toward one of the maintenance sheds.

"Sure." Jim stood up, brushed off his pants, and wiped his hands on a rag, which didn't do much for the oil stains on his fingers. Not that Frankie would have cared, if he could have gotten Jim's hands on him, stroking and caressing, tracing the bumps and dips of his spine. He would have stretched out like a lazy cat, basking in the attention.

They leaned against the side of the shed facing away from the base. It wasn't completely private but better than nothing.

"We lost George today," Frankie said, taking a drag and watching the smoke dissipate into the evening sunshine.

Jim grimaced. "Fuck. I'm sorry."

"Roy's taking it pretty hard."

"They were buddies, huh?"

"Yeah." Frankie flicked the ash off the end of his cigarette. "Did I ever tell you about Pete?"

Jim shook his head.

"He started off in our class, but he washed out after primary and transferred to bomber command as a navigator. He and I were good friends—well, we still are, I guess. We write to each other."

Jim's shoulders had grown stiff as Frankie spoke. "What do you mean? Were he and you…?"

"No." Frankie risked taking Jim's hand and stroking his wrist until Jim relaxed a little. "He had a girlfriend, and I never told him about my… my being queer. I had a bad crush on him, though. It tore me up when he got transferred."

Jim frowned and pulled his hand away. "So, what? Am I a... a replacement or something?"

"Of course not!" Frankie dropped the stub of his cigarette on the ground and twisted it under his heel. "Meeting you—dang it, Jim, it was the best thing that ever happened to me."

"Then why are you bringing this Pete fella up? Do you want me to tell you about the other guys *I* slept with?"

"No, I don't," Frankie snapped, jealousy flaring at the thought. "And that isn't why I mentioned Pete. We were just talking about friends, and he *is* my friend. That's not going to change."

"Great," Jim said flatly. "So you're writing letters to him, pining after him—"

"Dammit, I'm *not*! I don't want him anymore. It was just a stupid infatuation." Frankie pushed a hand through his hair, trying to think of what he could say to make Jim understand. "What we have—that's real. I'd be crazy to want anybody else when I have you."

Jim stewed over this for a moment and then said, "I don't like being your backup plan." He tossed his cigarette butt on the ground and started walking away.

Frankie grabbed his arm. "You're *not*. Would you just listen to what I'm trying to say?"

"I heard you. But anybody can talk pretty." The hurt he must have seen on Frankie's face made him pause a second, but then he shook his head. "I have to finish working on the plane."

Frankie watched him go in frustrated silence. If he could just pin Jim down and drown him with kisses, maybe that would convince him. But Jim probably wouldn't let him in his current mood, and it was a moot point anyway. Heaving a sigh, Frankie hunched his shoulders and wandered back to his barracks. He'd try to reason with Jim again when he got back from the mission tomorrow.

THE NEXT morning Jim didn't say much, his anger simmering, but he helped Frankie get strapped in, the same as always. Frankie just grunted his thanks, still sore at Jim's overreaction. Couldn't a guy have friends, for Christ's sake? It made him feel easier when Jim gave his helmet its usual tap, though.

His annoyance with Jim had helped him ignore his fear, but it surged to the fore as he moved into position for takeoff. Another strafing run today in France. He had on his parachute, but part of him had wanted to leave it behind. The certainty that he was going to get killed in that parachute, drifting in the air, the perfect target, had been settling into his bones, and he couldn't shake it. The cockpit seemed to close in around him, both a promise of safety and a trap from which he couldn't escape.

Muscle memory kept him flying when these thoughts overtook him, and by the time he had calmed down, they were over the coast of France. Frankie was a wing leader today for Blue Flight. Their entire squadron had been scrambled, and his flight hung near the middle of their formation. He checked their position and coordinates. Their orders were to break into smaller groups and hunt out likely targets once they cleared the Eure River.

As soon as they did, the order came from the squadron leader. Frankie's flight joined one led by Roy, and they started dropping closer to the ground, the better to spot likely targets. Heavy woods obscured the area, but they saw some train tracks, which had to lead somewhere. After a few minutes, the woods broke apart into a large open field that had been plowed and farmed at one point, but now had deep tire tracks tearing through the soil. Some kind of buildings stood at the far end, half-hidden under the trees.

Frankie never even saw the gun. He heard it first, the ack-ack of anti-aircraft fire spitting bullets into the air. He started to look, to turn, but it was already too late.

The metal and Plexiglas of the canopy splintered apart. Then the pain hit. It burned through his left arm and shoulder. Pain spiked in his left side, too, just under his ribs, but the sheer agony of his arm drowned it out. The plane veered wildly as a ragged cry tore from him, tears springing helplessly to his eyes. He struggled to steady the Mustang, but only his right arm obeyed his commands. His left arm hung limply, tremors of pain still traveling up and down the nerves.

Someone was yelling at him over the radio, but he couldn't spare the attention to answer, the words blurring meaninglessly together.

The altimeter started to drop. Some vital system on the plane had been hit. No telling how long it would remain airborne. Not to mention he couldn't fly with one arm. He had to bail out.

His mind took less than a second to rifle through those thoughts. As soon as it reached that conclusion, though, every muscle and limb froze in terror, only his heart still thudding desperately. If he bailed out... that anti-aircraft gun was waiting for him. It would fire on him the moment he inflated his parachute and hung helpless in the sky.

He would die if he bailed out.

He would die if he stayed in the plane.

Everything seemed so painfully clear for a second—the blood trickling down his wrist and staining his hand, the broken bits of glass littering the control panel, the smell of something burning, the needle slipping lower on the altimeter.

He didn't consciously move his right hand to unfasten the straps. He couldn't have made himself do it. But self-preservation overrode everything else, the instinctive desire to live, even if it was for just a few seconds longer.

He almost couldn't do it, even then. The pain in his left arm made him want to vomit, and he had to fight through it to flip the plane, pop the remainder of the shattered canopy, and release his straps. He tumbled free as gravity sank its claws into him. Scrabbling at his chest, he managed to rip the parachute cord.

The speed of his fall had scarcely registered before the straps jolted, the parachute puffing up with air and slowing him down. Pain rippled down his left side. He couldn't breathe, body prickling all over with terror, certain the bullets would hit him soon. But nothing happened, only the ground coming at him too quickly. A patch of trees loomed in his path. His left arm hung at his side, bent at a funny angle, throbbing. Weakly, he tried to maneuver the cords with his right hand. It wasn't enough, and he hit the trees, crashing down through the branches. Miraculously, he didn't get stuck and instead slammed into the ground inelegantly, only just managing to twist to his right side, taking most of the shock with his right leg.

Grass-blades pricked against his face. He lay there, breathing, marveling that he wasn't dead.

But he'd still been shot, and he was bleeding badly, shirt alarmingly sticky and wet where it stuck to his left side under his jacket. The parachute billowed around him, a silk shroud that threatened to entrap him. He managed to wriggle free of the harness and crawled a few feet, pushing the silk away, ripping and trampling it into the dirt.

Dizzy, the pain almost overwhelming him, he stopped, shuddering and taking deep, gulping breaths, his lungs burning from exertion.

Oh God, he couldn't go on like this. He was going to bleed out in this patch of forest.

Again terror brought a measure of clarity. He struggled out of his jacket, and this time he did throw up as he maneuvered his left arm free of the sleeve. Waiting a few seconds allowed the pain to subside to a more bearable level, enough that he could drag himself into a patch of shade. Bunching up the jacket, he pressed it against the wound in his side. Some shrapnel must have hit him—might still be in there for all he knew. He could only try to slow the bleeding.

Tears blurred his vision. He tried to move again but could only crawl a few feet before his strength gave out and the pain became too much.

Shaking, he sank down onto his back, staring up at the dark green leaves of the trees above him. If he was going to die, he wanted to spend these last minutes thinking of the best parts of his life. His mother and father. David. The mountains they could see from their ranch, drenched in a mellow sunlight on a late summer evening. Pete. Lifting off from the ground in a plane for the first time, before it had all gone to hell. And Jim. Christ, but he wanted Jim there with him.

He wasn't sure how much time passed. Blackness threatened to engulf him, and dream and reality merged, broken images confusing him. At some point he must have passed out, because he jolted awake to the sound of voices.

"Over here!"

"Hey, you okay, buddy? Damn, he's bled a lot."

Fingers at his throat.

"Still alive, though. Get Cooper over here."

He understood them. They were speaking English. That meant he'd come down behind the Allied lines. Thank God. He tried to open his eyes, blurry figures resolving into GIs crouched around him. One of them was a medic, filling a needle from a small glass bottle. He smiled at Frankie.

"I'm going to give you a shot, let you sleep. Trust me, you won't want to be awake while we move you."

Frankie didn't doubt that, the pain still a throbbing roar ebbing and flowing through his body. He shut his eyes again, welcoming the darkness.

CHAPTER SEVENTEEN

FRANKIE WOKE up an indefinite time later to the smell of wet canvas. It reminded him of camping trips when he was younger. In the summer he and his dad always went fishing at a lake about twenty miles from their ranch, camping out for a few days and feasting on trout. Sometimes David came with them. Sometimes one of his sisters. The tent always smelled like this in the morning, wet with dew. He would burrow down into the sleeping bag, listening to his dad building a fire.

His eyelids felt heavy, but he forced them open and slowly took stock of his surroundings. It *was* a tent, the same olive color as everything else in the Army. He was lying on a cot, an IV stuck in his arm. When he turned his head, he could see medical supplies stacked along the walls and other cots, although only one was occupied by a soldier who seemed to be asleep. The light was dim enough that it was either evening or not much past dawn.

His body seemed strangely numb and disconnected. The vivid memory of pain kept him from trying to move, although he was thirsty and wanted a drink of water.

Perhaps fifteen minutes later, an orderly ducked into the tent and noticed Frankie was awake.

"It's Frankie, right?" the guy said, smiling. They'd know his name from his dog tags, of course. "I'm Mitchell. How you feeling?"

Frankie tried to talk and finally made his mouth shape the right words to ask for water. Mitchell brought him some and held a straw to Frankie's lips.

"We've got you pretty doped up with morphine," Mitchell told him. "The medics had to operate right away when you were brought in by the patrol, and they stitched up your side. But we need to get you to a real hospital to deal with your arm. Multiple fractures, probably a torn tendon."

"When?" Frankie asked, only vaguely comprehending what Mitchell had said.

"We wanted to wait until you were stable and had some fluids in you. But we have regular transports going back to Britain, so it shouldn't be too long."

"My squadron—do they know I'm here?" Jim would have been waiting for him—sweating him out—and when Frankie didn't return, he'd assume the worst.

"Not sure. It's probably making its way through channels." Mitchell patted his good shoulder. "You're just lucky that patrol saw you go down and tracked your parachute."

"Tell them thank you. Please." It seemed so inadequate for people who had saved his life. But it was all he had. Frankie let his head fall back on the pillow, too exhausted to hold it up any longer.

"They'll just be glad to hear you pulled through. Too many don't."

Frankie watched as Mitchell went to check on the other guy and then started restocking a chest with medicine.

"Where are we?" he asked.

"About five miles outside of Mortain. The Germans have been pushing back hard the last couple of days, but we're holding."

Frankie tried to picture a map of France in his mind but was too drugged to manage it. Somewhere near the coast, he thought. "What day is it?"

"August eighth."

He'd lost about a day and a half, then, as he'd left the base on the sixth. Jim would definitely be thinking the worst.

He'd never told Jim plainly that he loved him. Wincing, he remembered the fight they'd had the evening before the mission. He should have said he was sorry. He should have said a lot of things. But now he'd been given the chance to do so.

THE TRANSPORT back to Britain was a blur of drugs and pain, first in a truck, then on a ship. They took him to a hospital in Cheltenham and did the surgery on his arm. Frankie finally ended up in an uncomfortable bed in the ward, his left arm in a sling, left side stitched and bandaged, aching all over and weak from the entire ordeal.

He knew this was it for him, in terms of the war. It would take weeks for the broken bones to heal and months to rehabilitate his arm. The doctors didn't know if he would ever achieve full flexibility or strength in his shoulder. It would be a long, long time before he ever flew a Mustang again and certainly not in combat.

Part of him was so fucking *relieved* about that, and it made the rest of him feel like a dirty coward. The dreams hadn't gone away, either. Instead, now he knew exactly what it felt like to be hanging in midair, dangling from a parachute. In his dreams, the anti-aircraft guns that had taken down his plane always got him, too, and he woke up on the edge of a scream.

Mostly, he thought about Jim. He was pretty sure word had gotten through that he'd made it and was in a hospital here. But this wasn't peacetime. Jim couldn't just rush off to see him at a moment's notice, although Fowlmere wasn't terribly far away. Sometimes he thought maybe Jim didn't want to come see him. He tried not to think it, because he remembered so well how Jim had kissed him and looked at him. But they had fought, and it was hard to keep such worries from consuming him in all the idle hours that filled the day.

It was maybe a week after the operation that the nurse told him he had a visitor. Frankie scrambled upright in bed, aware he hadn't brushed his teeth or combed his hair and his blue pajamas hung loosely on his frame. He'd lost a few pounds and was as skinny as he'd ever been.

Jim came through the door a few seconds later, eyes scanning the ward and finding Frankie. The smile that broke over his face was one of disbelieving joy, like he hadn't been sure Frankie was still alive until this moment. He jogged over, and Frankie reached for him, the first touch of Jim's hand on his arm such a wonderful warmth—and then they both froze, remembering they were in the middle of a hospital ward, surrounded by other people.

Jim still gave him a quick hug that Frankie clumsily returned with one arm, pressing his face into Jim's neck for just a second.

"Christ, but it's good to see you, Frankie," Jim said, sitting on the mattress and curling one leg under the other.

"Good to see you too." Frankie's throat felt tight, and he couldn't stop from tangling his fingers with Jim's, trying to hide the gesture under the covers.

"Roy told us you had been hit. He saw you going down, but he didn't know if you'd bailed out or not. I thought—" Jim stopped, shaking his head. "Your arm... are you...?"

"I won't be flying again anytime soon. But my side is healing—I got hit with some shrapnel—and it hasn't gotten infected. So I'm not going to die." He tried a smile, probably not a very good one, as the worried look on Jim's face didn't disappear. "I'm just stuck in bed for a while, and then they'll probably send me home to recuperate."

Jim nodded slowly. "I'm glad." He took a deep breath, looking away for a second. "I'm so glad you'll be out of it."

He couldn't tell Jim he felt the same sense of relief. He thought of Sergio, afraid of enclosed spaces but determined to serve in the Navy, determined to fight for men like them because no one else would. He should be like that. He should be upset he couldn't get back into the war.

Aloud, he said, "You get put with a new plane?"

"Yes. Some kid named Michael. Just as green as you were." He looked back, expression calm again. "Things are really heating up. We might be in Paris by the end of the week."

Frankie supposed he should feel jubilant, but he only felt tired. "That's swell," he made himself say.

Then, remembering, he reached over the side of the bed, sucking in a deep breath at the flare of pain but persevering. He dug in the bag that held the few sundry items he'd been issued, drew out two candy bars, and handed them to Jim. "Being in a hospital has its perks. I saved them, just in case you came by."

Jim met his eyes. "Did you think I wouldn't?"

Frankie shrugged, dropping his gaze to the blankets. "I know it can be hard to get a pass. And... well, I know you were angry at me."

"I was being stupid. Once I'd had a chance to think, I knew you weren't trying to make me jealous." Jim's voice grew softer, even though no one was listening to them, caught up in newspapers, card games, or with their own visitors. "When you didn't come back that day, I... I thought I was going crazy. I didn't know how I would...." He stopped, taking another steadying breath. "Goddamn it." He fished a pack of cigarettes out of his pocket and lit one.

"I'm sorry." He wasn't sure what he should be sorry for— doubting Jim, getting hit in the first place—but he was.

Jim smiled, his eyes sad. "Don't be. Just get better."

Better. He knew Jim meant more than just his arm. "I'll try. Jim...." He paused, not sure how to ask this. "They'll be sending me back to the States. When it's all over, will you... come and see me?"

Jim raised his eyebrows. "All the way to Kansas?"

It made him laugh, and Jim grinned, happier. "If you want me to come, I will."

"I do," Frankie said quickly. "But not if you're only doing it for me."

"Frankie." Jim waited until he looked at him. "I know you can be dense, but isn't it obvious that I love you?"

He couldn't speak for a minute, and he had to scrub away the tears threatening to fall. God, he'd never been so... fragile. "I feel the same," he choked out. "I love you too."

Jim gave him time to get himself under control, but when he met Jim's eyes, they were dark with everything he couldn't say or do. Frankie kind of wished he would just kiss him anyway, and damn the consequences.

"Do you have a pen? Some paper?" he asked Jim, who patted his pockets, searching. He did have a pen, but his only piece of paper was a train schedule. Frankie took it and squeezed the address of his parents' ranch in Idaho onto the margin.

"There." He handed it back to Jim. "That's where I'll be."

Jim tucked it away carefully.

Fumbling behind him, Frankie tried to push his pillow up so he could sit against the metal rungs of the bed. The movement pulled on his stitches, making him flinch. Jim helped, getting him settled, and then offered the pack of Lucky Strikes. "Here."

"Thanks." Frankie took one and held it out for Jim to light. Kind of hard to do when he only had the one arm.

"How bad is it? The pain, I mean."

"It could be worse. It *was* worse." Frankie shuddered, remembering.

He was glad when Jim changed the subject. "I've been practicing at Ping-Pong, you know. Next rematch, I'm going to beat you."

"Just keep on thinking that." Frankie closed his eyes, taking a drag. "I like my opponents overconfident."

Jim made a skeptical noise. "Just be glad you won't be on base tomorrow," he continued. "The Big Wheels are coming for a visit. Everything will have to be spit and polished. The CO has already got himself into a state."

"Sounds rough. Maybe you better go see the chaplain and get yourself a TS ticket."

"Oh, it's tough shit, all right." There was a pause, and then Frankie felt Jim plucking the cigarette out of his lax fingers. He'd been dozing off, even with Jim right next to him.

"Last thing we need is for you to set your goddamned bed on fire," Jim muttered. "You're tired, aren't you? And I should get going."

"No." It slipped out before Frankie could stop it. "Please stay. Just a bit longer."

"All right." Jim settled back down.

Frankie tried to watch him, because he didn't know how long it would be before he saw him again. But his eyes kept closing, his body still craving sleep despite not having done much else for the past week.

He woke some time later to a crick in his neck. Jim was gone, leaving a scribbled note and one of the candy bars. He squinted at the note. Jim had terrible handwriting.

*Had to catch the train and didn't want to wake
you. Eat this one yourself or a hard breeze is going to
blow you over.*

He ate the candy bar, even though he hadn't been feeling very
hungry of late, and he folded the note, putting it in his chest pocket
where it crinkled every time he moved.

CHAPTER EIGHTEEN

WAKING UP to the smell of pancakes cooking had stopped feeling surreal a few months ago, but he still sometimes had to lie in bed for a few minutes reminding himself he was back in Idaho and not on an airbase anymore. If it had been a good night, he could roll out of the warm blankets, get shaved, and go greet his ma with a smile and a kiss on her cheek. If it had been a bad night, it usually took at least twenty minutes before he could push down the residual panic, guilt, and shame and drag himself down to breakfast. His ma never said anything outright, but he could feel her worried eyes as he picked at his food.

This morning was one of the bad ones. In his dreams, he'd been back on a strafing mission. He could still feel the cold metal of the guns in his hands, see the small figures on the ground falling as he fired on them. The cockpit had exploded around him a few seconds later, just as it had happened in real life, only this time he couldn't get the canopy open, and thick smoke had surrounded him, choking him, blocking his lungs....

Shivering, Frankie scrunched his face into the pillow, taking deep breaths. At least, he thought grimly, his dreams provided some variety. It wasn't always that damned parachute signaling his coming death, although that nightmare remained the most frequent. After a few minutes, he snaked one arm from beneath the blanket's comforting warmth and reached over to the bureau. He had to use his right arm—his left couldn't handle such a long stretch. His left elbow still wouldn't straighten completely, and his shoulder ached almost all the time. Rebuilding the muscle strength would be a hard and painful effort his doctor had told him at his last appointment.

Fumbling on top of the bureau, he grasped the small stack of letters Jim had sent to him. Only six because the mail took a long time to get through the censors, though they had been apart eight months already. He had read and reread every one countless times.

He got the sense Jim was like David in not being particularly fond of writing. Each letter comprised little more than a page. Not like the two he'd had from Pete—he'd kept those as well—which carried on for three pages in an enthusiastic scrawl as opposed to Jim's cramped, laborious hand.

> *Frankie,*
>
> *Thanks for your letter and the chocolate. It didn't last long—the chocolate I mean. Hope your arm is on the mend and your mother is feeding you well. Real home cooking! I sure am jealous. If I never have to drink the swill that passes for coffee around here again, it will be too soon. I had a devil of a time the other day with the electrical system. Must have worked on it four hours, and the damn thing still went haywire within five minutes of liftoff. Went to the pub yesterday and drank a couple just for you. Have to run now because the fog is clearing, and we might get a mission off the ground after all.*
>
> *L Jim*

He imagined all the other things Jim might have written if it wasn't for the censors. At least, he hoped Jim had wanted to write stuff like that. As the months crawled along, he couldn't help but worry—maybe Jim had found someone else, perhaps his feelings for Frankie hadn't been as deep as he imagined. For his own part, none of the affection he felt for Jim had vanished. He missed him fiercely. Many times he regretted never getting a photo of Jim. As it was, he had to rely on his memory, which often led to him ducking into the bathroom, dick aching at the sense memory of Jim's mouth on it as he fumbled in his pants and jacked off desperately.

Laying the letters aside, Frankie ran a steadying hand through his hair and pushed aside the blankets. The late April nights were still cold—they'd even had some snow last week—but there was a tantalizing hint of spring in the air too. The longer days, the muddy yard, the catkins on the aspens all promised that soon winter would be swept away. He opened his curtain and looked out. The sun had been up a good long while, and he could see his dad and his little brother down by the barn, already working. He should have been out there helping, but his physical therapist had said he wasn't ready for strenuous labor yet, and his doctor said rest and relaxation would be best. He'd never told his doctor about the nightmares, but the man had probably guessed anyway. At the last appointment, he'd prescribed some sleeping pills, but Frankie refused to take them. He couldn't help thinking he deserved the nightmares on some level. If he hadn't been such a coward, he wouldn't be troubled by them, after all.

Frankie rested as much as possible, although moped might be a better term. He did some small jobs he could manage with just his right hand, but in truth, he didn't mind not being able to work on the ranch. He didn't want to settle back into the patterns that had dominated most of his life. He couldn't pretend nothing had changed, and he didn't want to. Next to missing Jim, he ached for the world that had been opened up to him—a world where he didn't have to always hide, where he had found other men like him, where being homosexual wasn't a sentence to isolation and shame.

A knock sounded on his door, and his ma said, "Frankie? Are you awake, honey?"

"Yep." Frankie cleared his throat and grabbed his bathrobe, shrugging into it, careful with his left arm.

The newspaper lying on the kitchen table carried more good news from Europe. Hitler's armies were crumbling. Paris had been liberated on the day before Frankie shipped out of Britain, and he remembered the celebratory mood in the hospital, the small contingent of French patients loudly singing "La Marseilles." He tried not to get too hopeful, though, tried not to start figuring out how long it might be before he could see Jim again. The Japs weren't surrendering, after all, and Jim might get shipped out to the Pacific. The fighting there didn't seem to be tapering down at all.

The last he'd heard from Pete, who had now been fighting the Japs for a year, had been word he was getting transferred to a desk job thanks to a bad case of smoke inhalation after their bomber had been hit. *Not too serious,* Pete had written, *and maybe I'll be able to return to the B-29 after a few weeks.* Frankie had been assailed with shame, knowing this was how you were supposed to behave. But instead of wanting to return to combat after his own injury, he'd been thankful he didn't have to fight anymore.

After breakfast he got dressed and put on his sheepskin jacket. "I'm going for a walk, Ma," he said on his way out, and she nodded, looking up from her ironing to give him a smile.

He hiked to a spot on the back corner of their property. A little creek wound its way through a thick clump of spruce trees, and a flat rock stood in the sunshine. He'd spent many hours here as a boy, reading comics, whittling sticks, and splashing in the creek. Sometimes David had been with him, but more often, he had come here when he wanted to be alone, escaping from whatever aggravations his siblings had visited upon him. He sat on the rock now, leaning his elbows on his knees. He'd been coming out here a lot, craving the solitude and the quiet.

He tried not to think about much while he was out here. It seemed... obscene, in a way, to bring the war into this place that brimmed with memories of his childhood, tainting something that should have remained unsullied.

Instead, he tried to turn his thoughts to the future and what he was going to do with himself. He supposed that was better than rehashing the war and his failures. It still made his chest heavy, though, because he knew he would never be able to fly again.

Physically, he could have done it. The PT was going as well as could be expected, and although his shoulder still hurt a hell of a lot sometimes where the bone had fractured, it was getting better. But mentally—emotionally—he knew he could never get back into the cockpit. Just thinking of it made him start to sweat, his stomach clenching, even as he longed for the sensation of speeding through the air, twisting and flipping, unbound by gravity. He'd lost that freedom—lost it forever. Thinking of it intensified the shame that had taken up permanent residence in his heart.

Jumping down from the rock, he dipped his hands into the stream, the freezing water burning and then numbing his skin. Jim knew he had been afraid, but everyone had been afraid. If he hadn't gotten injured, he probably would have fallen apart and had a nervous breakdown in the middle of the base for everyone to see. He almost welcomed the persistent pain in his arm for having spared him that humiliation.

What if Jim came back only to realize he no longer wanted Frankie, not like this?

He jerked his hands from the water and sank back into the grass, huddling in his coat and staring up at the sky.

WHEN HE got back to the house, his ma was talking to someone in the kitchen.

"Frankie, is that you?" she called out. "Come see who stopped by for a visit."

He shrugged out of his coat and walked down the hallway, hoping it wasn't Mrs. Kleinhauser. She was their closest neighbor to the east and made it a point to stop by at least once a week for a chat. No matter how busy you were, Mrs. Kleinhauser wouldn't leave until you'd made her a cup of coffee and sat down for a "real visit," as she put it. Sometimes his ma hid in the pantry when she saw Mrs. Kleinhauser's car coming down the access road. Since Frankie had been home, Mrs. Kleinhauser had taken to clipping out articles from magazines with advice on how to treat soldiers coming back from the front and dropping not-so-subtle hints about a psychiatrist in Boise who had completely cured her sister's husband's anxiety disorder. It made Frankie embarrassed, and his ma finally got so fed up she actually told Mrs. Kleinhauser to keep her nose out of other people's business. Mrs. Kleinhauser had left in a huff, but Frankie doubted she'd be put off for long.

But the girl sitting next to his mother at the kitchen table and smiling at him was not Mrs. Kleinhauser. Frankie stopped in the doorway, taking in her dark blonde curls and hazel eyes. "Ruth?" he said, shocked.

"Hi, Frankie," she replied, raising her hand in a little wave.

Ruth Baxter, his girlfriend from high school. God, it felt like a hundred years had passed since those days.

"Sit down, Frankie," his mother said, getting up and offering him the chair. "I'll leave you two to catch up. Those chickens won't pluck themselves."

Frankie sat down slowly, unsure of what to say.

Ruth watched him for a minute and then looked down at her coffee, swirling the spoon in the brown liquid. "I gave up hoping you'd visit and decided I'd better come here instead."

"I'm sorry." He cleared his throat. "I wasn't feeling very well for a long time and then, well, I guess I didn't realize you wanted me to visit."

Ruth shrugged. "I know we broke up, but that doesn't mean I hate you, Frankie. Lots of other people have been asking after you, too—Mary, Catherine, Esther, even Hank. You know, he couldn't enlist because of his asthma, but he's raised more money in war bonds than anyone else in town. I know he'd love to talk to you."

As she listed off their old classmates, a dull anxiety rose in Frankie's chest. He didn't want to see any of them. He didn't want to talk about his experiences in the war, for one, and he also didn't want to have to try and be the person they remembered from high school. He was done with that life.

"I just haven't been up to it, I guess," he muttered.

Ruth gave him a sympathetic smile. "Your mother is worried about you, you know. She thinks you spend too much time alone."

"Did she ask you to come?" he asked, struck with guilt. He didn't want his ma to worry, but of course she would. She'd watched him go off to war, confident and happy, and then he'd come back, weak, depressed, choking on the shame of how he'd behaved and trying to hide it from all the family and friends who looked at him and saw a brave soldier wounded in the line of duty.

"No. I wasn't lying when I said I wanted to see you." Ruth reached over and took his hand, and Frankie made himself hold still. "A bunch of us are going to Catherine's for a party on Sunday. Nothing fancy, just lunch and some games and music. You should come."

"I'll think about it."

She sighed and sat back, releasing him. "All right." He could tell she knew he wasn't going to come. But he couldn't muster the effort to put on a better pretense. If he went, he would have to joke with the guys and flirt with the girls. He could do it. Most of his life had been spent pretending he wanted a girlfriend, after all. But it felt like he would be betraying Jim if he did, and he couldn't do that, no matter what people thought.

"How have you been?" he made himself ask Ruth. It had been nice of her to come and see him, and he could be civil at the very least.

"I can't complain. I'm keeping busy with the Red Cross work and with the church. I just pray the war ends soon. Life has been so topsy-turvy these last years, and so many of our old friends are either serving or have moved away." She paused. "Did you hear about Dennis?"

"My ma told me."

Dennis Tate, valedictorian of their class, killed in the Pacific two weeks ago. With a class of only fifteen students, you knew everybody. Frankie had liked Dennis, although they hadn't been great friends. Dennis had never had a mean word to say about anybody, always unfailingly polite. Frankie recalled he'd been going steady with Mary and asked Ruth how she was holding up.

"She'll get better. It takes time." She gave Frankie a sad smile. "I guess you know all about that, though."

He could only nod.

"I bet you can't wait until David gets home, huh?" she continued, moving on to what she imagined to be a lighter subject. "I heard he was in some hard fighting on the Marianas but that he's okay."

"Yeah. Yeah, I can't wait to see him again." The words sounded hollow to him, but he wasn't about to tell Ruth what had happened.

A few more awkward minutes passed, and then Ruth finally stood up, saying she had to get going. "But I do hope to see you again soon, Frankie," she repeated.

"Thanks." He did smile then, because she had always been sweet, and that hadn't changed. "Say hi to everyone for me on Sunday, if I don't make it."

She promised she would, and he saw her to the door, then waved as she got in her car. Then he went up to his room and read all of Jim's letters again. Slumping back on his pillow, he shut his eyes, thinking about holding Jim in his arms. Then he remembered Ed and Junior and Dolly, joking and talking as they drove to San Diego that one weekend. He wanted to find that sense of camaraderie and shared experience again. He couldn't pretend it didn't exist and be content with hiding part of himself away forever.

CHAPTER NINETEEN

FRANKIE HEARD the news of Germany's surrender from the truck radio while driving back with his ma from a physical therapy appointment. The closest physical therapist lived in Twin Falls, a good three-hour drive from the ranch. His ma had driven him every week without fail, though, even when the weather wasn't so good and she'd had to negotiate icy roads. When the announcement had finished, she sagged forward for a second, the seatbelt catching her, before straightening again.

"Oh, thank God," she murmured. "Thank God." There was a catch in her voice, her eyes shining.

Frankie put his hand on her arm.

"If only we can end it in the Pacific soon," she said. "If only Colin doesn't get drafted." The tears spilled over, and she tried to wipe them away. "I'm just so thankful you're here with us. Whenever I think about how close I came to losing you...."

"Don't cry," he said, feeling awkward. He realized this was the first time his mother had ever talked about her fears with him. Usually she was upbeat, deftly taking care of the family. It made him realize he was an adult now, not a boy just out of high school who had rushed to join the Army, hardly thinking or caring about what the consequences might be.

Well, he knew a lot more about those now.

"I just couldn't bear having to watch Colin go through this too," his mother continued. "You're so brave, honey, and I know it's not easy for you."

"I'm not brave." His voice sounded stiff, horribly cold, and he tried to soften it. "I'll get better. I don't want you to worry about me."

It was true, and he vowed to make more of an effort to be cheerful, to engage with his family and not lock himself in his room or disappear for hours into the forest. "I know I haven't been very... pleasant to be around," he continued. "I'm sorry."

"Oh, Frankie. You don't have to apologize." She took a tissue out of her pocket and dabbed at her cheeks. "We all understand."

Maybe, but he needed to make more of an effort. He didn't want Jim to have to be around him like this. He needed to put together a plan, have a goal to work toward. Ruth's visit had made him realize he couldn't stay in his hometown. He'd be miserable, not to mention there was no way Jim could be with him, not surrounded by people who had known Frankie for years, who would ask all kinds of questions.

So, even as he began calculating how many days it might reasonably take for Jim to come back to the States if he wasn't sent directly to the Pacific, he started to think seriously about going to college. The Veteran's Administration had given him a bunch of pamphlets when he was discharged, and they explained how the government would pay most of his tuition and living expenses at a university. Maybe he could get into a college somewhere like San Francisco. He still remembered all of Junior's stories about the queer bars and clubs there.

He'd never thought seriously about college before. Too expensive, his grades weren't particularly good, and besides, he had been going to become a stunt pilot or a motorcycle racer. He felt kind of embarrassed at how shortsighted he had been, to be honest. He had a chance to really do something with his life now, not just end up as a ranch hand on some farm when he could no longer take the physical strain of stunt driving or flying.

So he sent for some applications, and his mother's smile grew brighter, and some of his guilt eased, even though he still had trouble sleeping.

By the end of July, he started to get anxious about Jim. More and more men were getting discharged, and with the Soviets ready to declare war on Japan and the constant, heavy bombardments visited on the island each week, everyone was feeling optimistic that

Japan's surrender might be on the horizon. Surely Jim wouldn't get sent there. Surely he would be discharged soon. He hadn't had any word from Jim, although it didn't surprise him. He could just picture the chaos of demobilization. Still. Maybe Jim had changed his mind. Maybe he wasn't going to come for Frankie after all.

He was in the post office one day in August, five days after Japan had surrendered, resigned to the discovery of only his father's subscription to *Field and Stream* in their box, when he turned around to find himself face to face with David's father.

"Mr. Buckley," he said, startled. Mr. and Mrs. Buckley had invited him over to dinner once, shortly after he returned home. It had been painfully awkward once it dawned on them Frankie hadn't heard from their son since they had both enlisted. Frankie had been miserable, reminded of all the dinners he had eaten here growing up, he and David conducting clandestine exchanges of candy and bubble gum—and, on one memorable occasion, a small frog—under the table.

"How are you doing, Frankie?" Mr. Buckley asked.

"Much better, sir."

"Good, good." Mr. Buckley studied him for a long moment, and Frankie knew he was wondering what had come between David and him. Apparently David had never said, and Frankie was grudgingly grateful for his silence.

"We expect David home before Thanksgiving," Mr. Buckley continued.

"He's all right, then?"

"Oh, yes. I'll be taking him on as a managing partner at the lumber store. Boy's more than earned it."

"Swell," Frankie said weakly, relief David had made it through warring with the fervent hope he would be out of town before he returned. God, it would be hell, running into David on the street and seeing the disgust and scorn in his eyes. "You'll give my best to Mrs. Buckley?"

Mr. Buckley nodded, frowning after him as Frankie escaped. He slammed the truck door shut behind him and gunned the engine, not caring if people stared as he sped down the street.

He woke up at 3:00 a.m. that night and couldn't fall back to sleep. Logically, he knew no one was going to burst in the door and demand he get his ass in gear because he was flying a mission at 0700 and better be ready. But his body was still tight with tension, reliving all the mornings when he *had* been going up and had to force himself to get into the cockpit.

Listless, he didn't get up until nine. His mother had saved a plate of breakfast for him, and she put her hand in his hair in silent sympathy. "Your father picked up a telegram for you when he was in town this morning," she said, handing him the slim piece of paper. "It came in late last night."

His heart froze and then sped up. He snatched it from her and tore it open.

WILL BE ON SATURDAY TRAIN 11 A.M. JIM

"What is it, honey?" his mother asked, probably perplexed by the grin splitting his face.

"A friend of mine from the squadron. He's coming to visit tomorrow." Frankie glanced up at her. "He might be here for a few days. Is that all right?"

"Of course. How wonderful that you'll have a visitor," she said, her voice warm, clearly relieved. She had never pushed him, even as she made it a point to mention various dances and card parties and luncheons where he would be sure to run into old classmates. "I'll plan a nice dinner."

He spent the rest of the day reliving every second he had spent with Jim, torn between a pervasive joy that tomorrow he would be with him again and an unshakable anxiety that maybe Jim's feelings had changed. It had been a whole year, after all. A whole year, with only a few letters to remind Jim he existed.

Frankie was at the station at ten-thirty the next morning, just in case the train arrived early. It ended up being twenty minutes late, and he paced up and down the platform, hands clenched in his pockets. When the whistle finally sounded, he took a deep breath

172

and then made himself lean up against the wall of the station house, trying to look casual and unconcerned.

He lost it the minute Jim stepped onto the platform. Jim looked the same as he remembered, dark hair shorn in tight locks around his ears, brown eyes lighting up as he spotted Frankie.

"Almost bought myself a ticket to Kansas—" Jim started to say, but Frankie pulled him into a tight hug, and Jim stopped speaking, startled. Before Frankie could get worried, though, Jim's arms wrapped around him too.

He didn't give a fuck if anyone thought it was too close an embrace for two men to be exchanging.

"I missed you," Frankie whispered. "So much."

"Hey, I'm here," Jim soothed, easing him away, although his hands remained on Frankie's shoulders. "Let me look at you."

The heat in his eyes, the familiar smile—Jim hadn't changed his mind, a year away hadn't dimmed their connection. Weak with relief, Frankie smiled helplessly, curling his hands around Jim's arms.

"Still a beanpole," Jim said, "but I like your hair a little longer like this."

"My ma keeps threatening to cut it, but I...." He blushed, just as awkward as he'd been their first night together. "I kept thinking you might like to have something to hold on to while I, you know," he finished in a whisper, his blush deepening.

"You're cute like this," Jim teased, "so embarrassed." Then his gaze grew more heated. "You think I never thought about it? Your mouth on me—*Christ.*" He gave Frankie's shoulders a squeeze. "Could hardly stand it, wanting you so much."

"Come on." Frankie pulled on his arm. "Let's get out of here." The desire to kiss Jim was overwhelming. He didn't know how long he could hold out. "My truck's this way. You got all your gear?"

"Yeah, not much to it. They wouldn't let me keep the plane."

"Shame, that." Frankie slowed a little so he could touch Jim's hand again, look at him, and try to convince himself Jim really was here.

173

"I poured gallons of sweat into that Mustang," Jim complained, but a little smile wrinkled the corner of his eyes as he watched Frankie. "You'd think that would be worth something, but I guess not."

"I'll help you forget about it," Frankie promised, more lighthearted than he had been since—well, since the last time he had seen Jim. "I'll give you something else to occupy your mind." He took Jim's duffel and tossed it into the back of the truck.

"I won't say no to that offer." Jim clambered into the passenger seat and propped one foot on the dashboard. "This really is the sticks, isn't it?" he commented, as he looked around, taking in the small town.

"City boy," Frankie teased, pulling out of the parking lot and then rumbling down the street.

"Sure is nice and quiet, though." Jim leaned back, closing his eyes. "I spent most of the train ride here asleep. These last few weeks, it was just go, go, go. God, I'm glad to be shot of that whole outfit."

"Army life not your style, huh?"

"You know it isn't. I like sleeping in, for one thing."

Frankie glanced over at him. "You can take a nap, if you want. I have stuff I can do, and we can talk more later—"

Jim sat up, opening his eyes. "Are you kidding me? I've waited an entire year to get you to myself again. I'm not sleeping a wink until I've at least kissed you."

"Good." He didn't say anything else, just waited until they were far enough outside of town before yanking the wheel to the side and pulling off the road. Jim yelped, but quickly caught on as Frankie parked the truck under some pine trees. As soon as he had killed the engine, Jim crawled across the seat, contorted his limbs until he managed to straddle Frankie's lap, and squeezed in between Frankie and the steering wheel.

"Finally," Jim panted, seizing his mouth in a hungry kiss. He had the top button undone on Frankie's shirt, and Frankie pulled Jim's shirt out of his pants, warm skin meeting his seeking hands.

Frankie could hardly catch his breath, could hardly tear his lips away from Jim's, but he had to say it. "I love you. Jim. I love you."

"Love you too. Christ, Frankie." Jim's hips were moving, rutting against Frankie's stomach, so beautifully desperate. Frankie struggled with his belt, trying to get it undone. Jim put out a hand to steady himself as he leaned back to give Frankie better access and ended up pressing the horn by mistake. It blared a loud, long honk.

"Shit!" Jim startled to the side, falling half-off Frankie's lap. Frankie jumped a little, and his left arm banged into the door, shoulder flaring with pain for a second.

They looked at each other, and Frankie started laughing. Jim joined him a second later.

"You almost bit my tongue," Frankie gasped.

"Sorry, but it was a tight fit. That blamed wheel—I didn't exactly *care* at the time, but still. Ouch." Then his eyes lit up. "Wait. This is a truck. With a bed. A *bed.* It's almost too perfect."

Frankie gaped at him a moment and then pushed his door open and tumbled out. Jim scrambled out the other side.

"Will anyone see?" Jim asked as Frankie pulled down the tailgate and hopped up.

"No, we're far enough out, and not many people drive this road." He paused, looking at the hard metal. "There's no blankets or anything."

"Does it look like I give a shit?" Jim demanded, climbing up beside him. He was all over Frankie again the next second. "But you go on top—your arm—"

"It's fine," Frankie insisted, but he didn't protest, not when his hips were slotting so comfortably between Jim's thighs, not when Jim's mouth was back on his, and his hands were deftly opening Frankie's shirt and pushing it away.

Jim's fingers turned gentle when he found the scars. Frankie kissed his neck, closing his eyes and shivering at the light touch.

"Your arm," Jim said softly, "could you still manage the controls?" He didn't have to specify of what.

175

"I could, but...." Frankie's voice sank, and he tried to block out everything except Jim's scent and warmth. "I can't fly again. I can't."

Jim didn't ask any more questions, just coaxed Frankie up into another kiss.

Their earlier urgency had faded somewhat, but it didn't take long before both of their trousers were pushed down around their thighs. They rocked together, and Jim's palms slid down to cup Frankie's ass. Frankie couldn't stop saying Jim's name in between groans and frantic breaths. They were too wound up to last long, even if Frankie wished it could go on forever, the two of them twined together like this. Jim came first, a splash against Frankie's stomach, and then worked a hand in between them to bring Frankie to completion too. When he came, he muffled his cries in Jim's shirt, mouth pressed against Jim's pounding heart.

His arms gave out a second later. He slumped his full weight onto Jim's chest, the sparking remnants of his orgasm still flaring up his spine.

Jim gave him a minute, resting his hand between Frankie's shoulders, but then he started wriggling. "Up. Off."

Frankie rolled to the side, uncoordinated, watching as Jim sat up. He sure looked nice—lips red and swollen, shirt pushed up around his armpits, a trail of come in the dark hair around his groin.

"Next time, there is going to be a mattress," Jim announced, rubbing at his back and wincing.

"Sorry." Frankie flopped a contrite hand onto his thigh and squeezed.

Jim grinned down at him. "I see I'm going to have to work on your stamina."

Frankie would happily submit to whatever training Jim wanted to give him. First, though—"We need to get back." He yawned, rubbing his thumb above Jim's hipbone. "My mother's making dinner."

Jim blinked down at himself. "Damn. One look at us and it's going to be pretty obvious what we've been up to."

"Nah." Frankie kept stroking, inching closer to Jim's softening cock. "We'll stop at the creek and wash up."

Jim caught Frankie's hand. "Now, baby, let's not get carried away. I don't want to offend your mother by being late."

Frankie sighed but relented and gave Jim a last kiss before scooting down to the tailgate and dropping to the ground. He pulled up his pants, scrubbing at the come drying on his stomach and decided to put his shirt on after he'd washed it off.

As soon as Jim got down, though, he had to pull him back into a hug. "Thought I might never see you again," he mumbled into Jim's hair.

Jim hugged him back, careful of Frankie's arm. Then he ruffled his hair and pulled away. "Let's go. I'm hungry as a horse. I can't remember the last time I had a nice home-cooked meal."

Frankie let him go reluctantly, got back into the driver's seat, and started the engine. They managed to erase the most obvious evidence of their activities before going to the ranch, and his mother's smile was nothing but welcoming when she opened the door for them. Frankie introduced Jim, and his mother ushered them into the sitting room, bringing coffee and a plate of cookies.

"Won't these spoil my appetite?" Jim asked, grinning.

"If you're anything like Frankie and my other son, you'll have no problem with it," she replied, and Jim happily gobbled several.

His father and brother arrived a short while later, and there were introductions and desultory chit-chat about Jim's work as a mechanic.

"Frankie didn't mention you were his crew chief," his mother said on one of her trips between the kitchen and sitting room with more coffee.

"Probably 'cause I gave him hell all the time," Jim replied, unfazed. "What about you, kid?" He turned to Colin. "You as crazy as your brother?"

Colin slid a guilty look at their mother. "Well...."

"He has his moments," Frankie's father said, dry as always.

It felt strange to have Jim sitting at the dinner table with them, politely asking his father to pass the potatoes and salt. And it was hard not to give Jim meaningful looks, particularly when Jim kept bumping his leg under the table with his foot.

"I sure appreciate all this, Mrs. Norris," Jim said as he scraped the last bit of potatoes off his plate. "I hope it isn't an inconvenience for you."

"Of course not," she replied. "You're very welcome in our home. I know Frankie was so pleased you were coming to visit." She paused and turned to Frankie. "Where is Jim going to sleep, honey? Colin is in your sisters' old room, and I don't trust that dreadful old cot not to break in the middle of the night."

"He can bunk with me," Frankie replied. "We're used to tight quarters in the Army."

"If you're sure," his mother said to Jim, sounding apologetic.

"That will be fine," Jim assured her. "I'll give him a good whack if he snores too loud."

They ended up on the back porch after dinner, Frankie's parents in the kitchen doing the dishes and Colin listening to the radio. Jim leaned on the railing for a while, taking in the view, and then came to sit next to Frankie. He lit a cigarette. "So. Here I am."

"Here you are." He risked leaning over and kissing Jim's temple.

Jim leaned into the caress, smiling. "Just how quiet will we have to be tonight?"

Frankie considered. "Pretty quiet. My brother is in the room next to us, and my parents are just down the hall."

Jim nodded. "I can do quiet." He tilted his chair back. "Think there are any of those cookies left?"

"I'll check." Frankie went into the kitchen.

"What do you need, honey?" his mother asked.

"Jim wants another cookie."

"Why don't you give him some of that cake I baked on Wednesday? There should still be a slice or two left, unless Colin ate it. I swear, that boy is a bottomless pit—twice as bad as you ever were."

Jim's eyes lit up when Frankie returned with a piece of chocolate cake and a fork. "Didn't you want any?" he asked, accepting them and taking a bite.

"Nah. I'm full from dinner."

Jim gave him a dubious look. "You're still too skinny. I thought all these months would have put some meat on your bones."

Frankie didn't reply. He knew he was too thin and too pale, but he hadn't had much of an appetite. He had felt more like himself these past few weeks, and never better than he had today, but he couldn't shake the nightmares or the persistent humiliation at how he had fallen apart on the missions. He was going to have to tell Jim about it, confess to the things Jim might have guessed at but hadn't known for sure. Jim deserved to know. Frankie couldn't ask him to stay without making it clear being with him wasn't going to be a picnic. If Jim would even want to be with him once he realized what a coward Frankie had been.

The sound of Jim's fork scraping against his plate brought him back to the present. Jim put his plate down with a happy sigh. The last light had left the top of the ridge, and the mountain air had started to become chilly. Jim pulled his jacket closer. "If it was a little warmer, I'd call this paradise."

Frankie pretended to be hurt. "My presence alone isn't enough for you, huh?"

Jim raised his eyebrows. "Frankie, I love you, but cold feet are cold feet, no matter how you slice it."

"We'll have to get you some wool socks. And a leather jacket—didn't I promise you one of those?"

Jim's smile grew softer, pleased. "You remember that?"

"Of course." Only having those few days to dwell on had made every second infinitely more precious. "I should have had one waiting for you, but you didn't give me much advance notice you were coming."

"Sorry." Jim looped his fingers together, looking down at them. "I almost didn't come," he admitted quietly. "Not because I didn't want to," he hastened to add, "but I was afraid maybe you didn't want me to anymore. It was so long since I had seen you."

The admission made him flinch, but he tried to put aside the instinctive panic and anger. "I was scared too," Frankie told him, putting his hand over Jim's. "But I never stopped wanting you, Jim. Not once."

Jim squeezed his hand, and they fell silent, sitting on the porch until full night had fallen, and they could see the stars. "Ready for bed?" Jim asked at last, his voice low.

Swallowing, Frankie nodded, lust kindling warmth into his limbs. They slipped up the stairs and locked the door of Frankie's room behind them.

"Have to be quiet," Frankie whispered, bending over Jim and cupping his face in his hands. They kissed slowly this time, hands brushing along each other's bodies, relearning their shape and texture.

"Do you remember what I asked you?" Jim breathed next to his ear. "Do you remember what I wanted you to do to me?"

Frankie sucked in a breath and curled his arms more tightly around Jim. "Yes."

"Say it," Jim demanded, and then he sucked on Frankie's earlobe, startling a moan out of him.

"You wanted me to fuck you."

Jim hummed in approval. "I still want it. Think you can do that for me, baby?"

"God, yes. Anything." He carded his fingers through Jim's hair, kissing his forehead, his cheeks, and his mouth.

Jim started unbuttoning his shirt, and Frankie stumbled over to his table. He searched for a match and lit the oil lamp. When he turned back, Jim was bare-chested and had already moved on to unbuckling his belt. Frankie just stood there, watching appreciatively as Jim shucked off his trousers and shorts. His thick cock wasn't completely hard yet, but it curved away from his body. Jim reached down and gave it a few lazy tugs, grinning at the look on Frankie's face.

"I'm just gonna stretch out here," he said, moving to the bed, "and enjoy the view."

Frankie blushed again as Jim lay down, hand still fondling between his legs, dark eyes intense. He forced himself to move slowly as he unbuttoned and took off his shirt, thumbed the buttons of his trousers before opening them, then bent down and turned to remove his shoes and socks so Jim got a nice look at his ass.

"Now come here," Jim ordered roughly once Frankie was naked.

He obeyed, sighing as their skin slid together, sinking into Jim's arms. Jim dropped kisses along his collarbone, fingers skimming Frankie's sides. When their cocks brushed together, Frankie jerked like he'd been shocked.

"Tell me what to do. Please, Jim. I don't know how, and I want this to be good for you." It didn't embarrass him now to admit to his inexperience.

Jim petted his back soothingly. "Do you have any Vaseline?"

"In the bathroom. Hang on a minute." He grabbed his robe, and ducked out into the hall, praying he didn't run into Colin or his parents. The hallway remained empty, and a minute later he was back in the bed, seeking and finding Jim's warmth again.

Jim kissed him, and then he turned onto his stomach and spread his legs. "Get your fingers slick and then...." He cleared his throat and turned his head so his next words were a little muffled by the pillow. "Just stick them in me. Start with one and build up to two or three."

Frankie could see the flush on Jim's ears. "Hey," he whispered, rubbing his hand along Jim's spine. "You're so gorgeous like this."

Jim relaxed on a sigh, resting his head on his arm so he could look back at Frankie. "This is my first time too," he said, smiling. "Guess I'm nervous."

"Don't be. If I do something wrong, just tell me, and I'll stop."

Jim nodded and then gestured to the Vaseline. He licked his lips. "Go on."

Blood rushing in his ears, cock aching, Frankie slicked his fingers and knelt between Jim's legs. He touched his sack first, stroking the sensitive skin, and then slid his fingers up, spreading Jim's ass a little with his other hand. Jim made a noise when he touched the ridged, taut skin around his hole, but it sounded like a good noise. Frankie rubbed his finger there, then held his breath and pushed inside.

Jim clenched around him, so tight, and Frankie froze. He circled his thumb in the soft flesh of Jim's ass. "Okay?"

Relaxing again, Jim nodded, so Frankie pushed his finger in farther and then drew back. He slid in deeper, and Jim made a noise like he'd been punched. "Sorry, sorry," Frankie said, starting to pull out, but Jim reached back and grabbed his arm.

"No. No, do it again. It felt good. Really good."

So Frankie did, and Jim moaned, pushing back to meet him. "Try another finger," Jim gasped.

Two fingers really lit Jim up, and he stuffed the pillow in his mouth, biting down on it to keep quiet. He was rubbing his cock against the sheets, in time with the rhythm Frankie had set. Frankie had to use his other hand to squeeze his own cock at the base, so desperately close to coming at the way Jim looked, at the way he felt around his fingers.

"Jim," he breathed. "Can I, please?"

Jim spat out the pillow long enough to say, "Yes. Fuck, yes." Frankie slicked his own cock and then spread Jim's ass again. Just the touch of his cockhead against Jim's hole was enough to almost do him in, and he had to stop a second, holding his breath. Jim tilted his hips back farther, getting onto his knees, trying to draw Frankie inside.

When he got a grip on himself, Frankie nudged his cock forward, trying to go slow. There was a lot of resistance at first, but then he was past it, and he slid farther, faster than he had intended.

"Wait, wait," Jim said, shaking, and Frankie stopped, hands gripping Jim's hips hard enough to bruise. He waited, feeling as Jim unclenched his muscles and adjusted to Frankie's cock spreading him wide. "All right," Jim finally said, and Frankie shuddered, tension unspooling as he drew back slightly and fucked deeper.

He didn't have any finesse, that was for sure. And he probably went too fast, thrusting into Jim, pleasure twining up his spine and narrowing his focus to Jim's scent and flexing muscles. He pressed his nose into the back of Jim's neck, arms tight around his chest.

Jim's breathing grew more and more ragged, and when Frankie came, unable to hold back any longer, Jim groaned, slumping down onto the bed.

Frankie tried to hold up his weight so he didn't crush Jim, and they ended up on their sides, spooned together. His cock slipped out, and he hastily fumbled his hand there instead, feeling Jim's slick skin, stroking a finger just inside his swollen entrance.

Jim made a startled noise and then grabbed at his cock, pumping it in his fist. Frankie craned his neck, going up on one elbow so he could kiss him, catching the sounds Jim made as he came.

"Love you," he whispered.

Jim sank back against his chest, smiling. "Pretty hard not to, huh?" he mumbled. His eyes were shut, and he sounded sleepy and sated.

Frankie huffed a quiet laugh and kissed his shoulder. They were sweaty and sticky, but he couldn't bring himself to move for a few long minutes. Finally he scrabbled for his shirt on the floor and tried to clean off some of the come and Vaseline.

"How do you plan to explain that to your mother?" Jim asked, cracking open an eye.

"I'll wash it myself. Or bury it."

Jim laughed, shaking with mirth, and twisted around for more kisses. He reached down, trying to get the blankets, and Frankie helped him pull them up.

"Stay close," Jim ordered. "Keep me warm." He yawned. "Feels like winter, I swear."

"It can get pretty cold overnight," Frankie admitted, but he didn't feel too sorry for Jim, not if it meant he got to keep his arms tight around him as they drifted to sleep.

HE HAD to spend an anxious few minutes in front of the bathroom mirror the next morning, checking to make sure Jim hadn't left any visible marks on him. A turtleneck sweater in August just couldn't be explained. But Jim had kept the kisses gentle around his throat. Meeting his eyes in the mirror, Frankie smiled, feeling giddy. He practically skipped down the stairs and gave his ma a big hug when he came into the kitchen.

Jim was already sitting at the table, a big stack of pancakes in front of him. He smirked at Frankie's good mood, obviously taking all the credit for it himself. As he should. Frankie sat beside him, helping himself to some bacon.

"Well, aren't you two chipper this morning," his mother commented, turning the pancakes on the griddle. She smiled at them, free of suspicion, and Frankie said a silent prayer of thanks she hadn't caught on to what was between him and Jim.

They lingered at the breakfast table, telling his ma they would take care of the washing up. They didn't say much, just basked in the memories of the night before.

"I'll get fat if I stay here much longer," Jim commented when they finally roused themselves and had heated enough water to do the dishes.

Frankie's heart started thudding a little louder, and his contentment dissipated in a surge of anxiousness. "We wouldn't have to stay here much longer," he began cautiously, and Jim paused, hands stuck in the soapy water. He looked at Frankie.

"I applied to college," he continued, and Jim raised his eyebrows, surprised. "San Francisco State. I'm starting in January. I would have written, but with the squadron getting decommissioned, I didn't know where to find you."

"College," Jim said slowly. "Didn't figure you for the type."

"Neither did I, but, well, things change." He concentrated on drying the plate in his hands, then set it on the shelf. This was the moment, the time to tell Jim everything. He had to do it.

"I still have... bad spells, Jim. Especially at night. I know I never talked about it, but toward the end there, I was getting pretty messed up."

Jim slowly rinsed off a glass. "Frankie, I watched you force yourself into that plane every morning. I know how hard it was."

He knew. Jim had known. Ashamed, Frankie looked away, twisting the towel in his hands. "I was such a coward," he choked. "I was *glad* to get injured, glad to be out of the war."

"You were brave." Jim's voice was hoarse, and he had stopped scrubbing the pan, although he kept his eyes on the sink. "You were so fucking brave. Don't ever think otherwise."

Frankie didn't—couldn't—believe him. "But I was so afraid, Jim. And I... can't fly anymore," he admitted in a whisper. "I'm still too scared to ever get into a plane again."

Jim drew his hands out of the water, dried them, and then pulled Frankie into a hug. "I'm sorry. I know you loved it."

He was going to start crying. Furious at himself, he rubbed at his eyes, pressing closer to Jim.

"Everyone was afraid, Frankie," Jim continued. "But you never gave up, did you? Even when you were so scared, you never backed out of a mission."

"I couldn't have kept going much longer, though. I thought I was going to break down, start having hysterics right there on the runway." Sniffing, he drew away, slumping against the counter. "Still feel that way sometimes."

Jim nodded and reached out to thumb along Frankie's jaw and then around the back of his neck. He rested his hand there, warm and solid. "I love you."

Frankie looked up, studying Jim's face. His eyes were open, honest, laden with affection. It seemed too good to be true, that Jim was willing to deal with all of Frankie's shit, that he loved him despite the ways the war had damaged him. "Love you too," he managed, throat almost too tight to speak.

Jim gave him a little shake and then turned back to the dishes. Dazed, Frankie dried them as they got washed and mechanically put them in their places.

"So, San Francisco," Jim said after a few minutes.

"Yes." Frankie made himself focus, alert to the slight hesitation in Jim's tone. "And I want you to come with me."

Jim's smile was slow, almost private. "I always thought it sounded pretty nice, there by the bay." He nudged Frankie's boot with his shoe. "Although, I guess I wouldn't mind anywhere, so long as you were there."

Frankie smiled back, relief and happiness singing through him. "Sweet talker."

"What exactly are you going to do in college?" Jim asked as he washed the last dish.

"Get a teaching license."

"Teaching?" Jim paused, surprised again. "As in the kind of teaching where parents trust you with their children?"

Frankie glared. "Yes."

Jim snorted. "God help us."

"I like kids," Frankie protested. "And I may not be that smart, but I'm pretty sure I can teach fifth graders about math and geography."

"You're going to have those kids testing explosives in chemistry and building balsa wood gliders. Don't lie."

"Well, I might have considered a few experiments like that, stuff *we* never got to try in school because Mrs. Wells had a big stick up her—" Frankie stopped, unable to keep from grinning at how hard Jim was laughing.

Maybe he had lost some things in the war. Maybe he had emerged damaged and stuck to the earth, the vast sweep of the sky closed to him. But he'd gained something too—the knowledge he wasn't alone and never would be. He wasn't a weird abnormality but one of many. And he'd found Jim.

It was enough—more than enough—to keep going on.

SELECTED BIBLIOGRAPHY

Bérubé, Allan, *Coming Out Under Fire: The History of Gay Men and Women in World War II*

Curtis, Richard K., *Dumb But Lucky!: Confessions of a P-51 Fighter Pilot in World War II*

Fortier, Norman "Bud", *An Ace of the Eighth: An American Fighter Pilot's Air War in Europe*

Kaiser, Charles, *The Gay Metropolis: The Landmark History of Gay Life in America*

Vrilakas, Robert A., *Look, Mom—I Can Fly!: Memoirs of a World War II P-38 Fighter Pilot*

R.A. THORN lives in northern California, although her heart remains in the Colorado mountains. She enjoys exploring the strange and varied paths of history, whether in her fiction writing or more scholarly pursuits. In her writing she seeks to capture the elusive feeling of a particular historical period and the way its people thought and felt. Many days find her sequestered in the archives or pursuing the odd historical fact, but when chance allows, she likes to escape and go hiking. She is perhaps too fond of footnotes and dark chocolate and looks forward to the day when she can get a dog.

Website: http://romanceofthepast.com

Memory

DOUG LLOYD

http://www.dreamspinnerpress.com

The Quality of Mercy

J.S. COOK

http://www.dreamspinnerpress.com

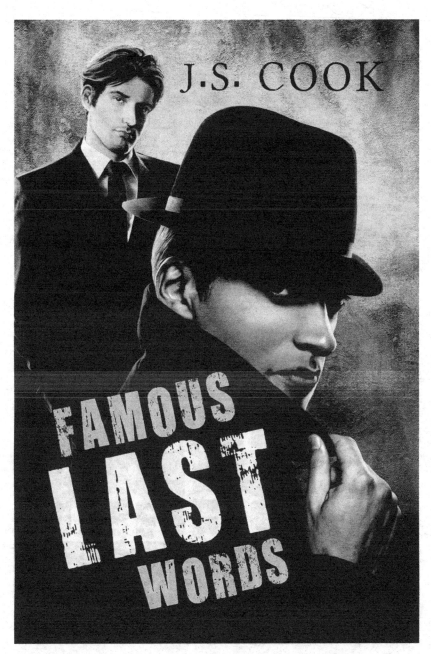

J.S. COOK

FAMOUS
LAST
WORDS

http://www.dreamspinnerpress.com

Rival
Within

SJD PETERSON

http://www.dreamspinnerpress.com

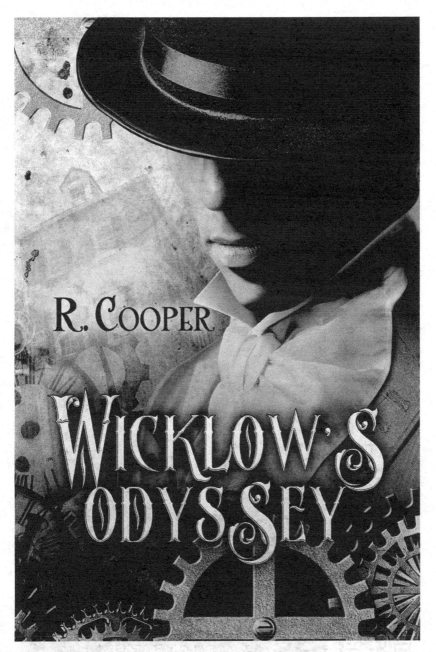

R. COOPER

WICKLOW'S ODYSSEY

http://www.dreamspinnerpress.com